THE SHADOW BEFORE

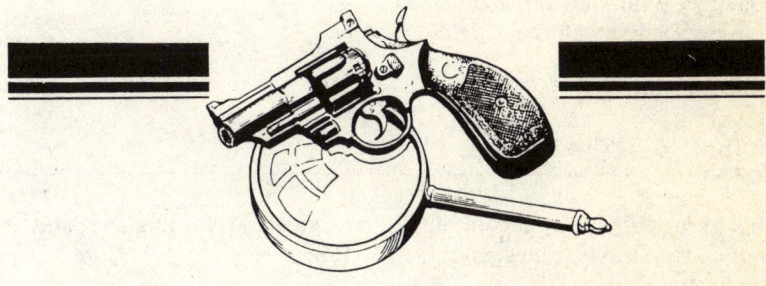

John Newton Chance

ATLANTIC LARGE PRINT

Chivers Press, Bath, England.
John Curley & Associates Inc.,
South Yarmouth, Mass., USA.

Library of Congress Cataloging in Publication Data

Chance, John Newton.
 The shadow before / John Newton Chance.
   p.   cm.—(Atlantic large print)
 ISBN 1-55504-840-4 (pbk.: lg. print)
 1. Large type books.   I. Title.
[PR6005.H28S53 1989]   88-35026
823'.912—dc19   CIP

British Library Cataloguing in Publication Data

Chance, John Newton, *1911–1983*
 The Shadow before
 I. Title
 823'.914 [F]

 ISBN 0-7451-9461-3

This Large Print edition is published by Chivers Press, England, and John Curley & Associates, Inc, U.S.A. 1989

Published by arrangement with Robert Hale Limited

U.K. Hardback ISBN 0 7451 9461 3
U.S.A. Softback ISBN 1 55504 840 4

© John Newton Chance 1988

CHAPTER ONE

1

The man was distraught. I could tell that by the curiously tense yet toneless quality of his voice. His speech was a low monotonous sound, but with every word clear to me, sitting in the next cubicle.

I could have turned my head and seen the speaker and his companion, but I felt I dared not in view of the words that came first to my ears.

The cubicle divisions were only three feet high. My Straight Malt whisky might have stayed untasted, I was so appalled by the words the man was saying. I remember them now, almost perfectly.

'I've thought this out all the way through, Mac. Right through. Days—weeks. Right through. I shall kill her. There just isn't any other way. She won't let me find another way, so she'll have to go. I can't live like this any longer.'

'Cool it, old man. Cool it.'

'I'm dead cool now, Mac. I've been cool for weeks now. You see, where you can't understand is where you don't know. You don't know how my life has been these last years. You don't know the humiliations she's piled on me, day after day—all the bloody time—'

'It's a phase, Jim,' Mac said quietly. 'All marriages go through rough patches. You must—'

'Phases don't last years. Rough patches are things you hit on together. Accidental. You don't have a wife setting out to destroy her husband over three years. You just don't know. You think it's another man come on the scene, probably. If it was that, I'd try and understand, but it isn't that. It isn't anything like that. This is deliberate. Cold-blooded. She laughs at me. She makes everybody else join in. Deliberately. She is destroying me, Mac. That's what she's doing, and she enjoys it. It's appalling how much she enjoys it—'

There was a silence. I wished Julia would arrive. There was no other cubicle left now. We, the two and I were at the end of the row.

It was odd how clear the despairing voice sounded. As if the noise of the long bar was tuned down to let him speak. As if it were taking place in a film, where the director eased the background noise down when the man spoke.

I watched the entrance. Julia was late. But the traffic was thick out there. The cab might be having a job getting through.

'You can't have thought it through, Jim. There's divorce. Surely you've got grounds—'

'What makes you think divorce is feasible

2

now? You know that side of the situation, Mac. You know it well enough. There really is just the one way, and I do know how—'

'Jim, cool it. Things may be bad right now, but you have to think of the years ahead of you. You're both only thirty-four. You can't throw away the rest of your life thinking of murder. That's what it is, Jim. That's the real word for it. I don't think you can realise—'

'No, it's you can't realise, Mac. You.'

'But if she's been unfaithful—'

'Unfaithful! You've got the wrong word altogether, Mac. Dead wrong. Unfaithful? Yes, maybe once, twice, three times even. Unfaithful!' With that word a slight rising of tone came into his voice and he laughed with bitterness that hurt me to hear.

'Look, Jim. Whatever it is she's done, you—'

'Hold it there, Mac. Do you know what she's doing? Have you heard nothing about it? Nothing at all? Do you swear to me you haven't heard any whisper—?'

'Keep your voice down, man!'

There was a pause.

'Don't you know, Mac?'

'One hears gossip.'

I watched the door in the distance, wishing she would come. When she did come, I'd take her to some other place. I wanted to go, but I could not stop listening. I drank my Scotch, tried to read my paper, but the level

3

grey voice kept on.

I began to feel, like Mac, that I should get up and tell the man not to do it. Not to let himself be wrecked by his belief the only way out of his torture was by killing.

Because I could feel in my heart that he was going to do it. I began to wonder whether I might take some official step to stop him . . .

'One hears gossip,' he said.

'What gossip, Mac? That she's playing fast and loose? Something like that? Something quite simple like that? Is that what you've heard? You're out of date, Mac. That's what she used to do. That's the way she used to drive me mad. But not now.'

'All right, Jim. She's a nymphomaniac. Women sometimes can't help things like that. It's part of their make-up—'

'She's not nympho, Mac. That would mean a bit of heat in her. She hasn't got any. She's dead cold. The pleasures she gets are from humiliation. From cruelty. From sadism. I tell you, Mac, though you won't believe it, she's a very extraordinary character. She can wreck anybody just for the pleasure of seeing them squirm—'

'Jim, cool it, I tell you. Don't start on the old pulling-the-legs-off-flies routine. Don't start making things up, because that may be what's getting you now.'

'Let me give you a little example, Mac. You know our neighbourhood was top-class once, but now it's getting to be as dangerous as any other place near the city? I had a spy-hole put in the door because of night callers.

'She doesn't use it. Geraldine doesn't use it. No. Geraldine goes to the door with a bloody chopper and opens the door hoping it is some mugger who's ringing the bell. Now think of that, man. Just think of that attitude, and then get your ideas into a new perspective.'

'What do you mean a chopper? Not a thing you split wood with—'

'That's just what it is, Mac. A small axe for splitting firewood, and heads, she hopes. She would, Mac. She would, if a man came there and threatened her, she'd cut his head in half—and like it.'

'Easy, Jim. Nobody's going to believe that of her, you know. You must cool it. You're making me feel—'

'Okay. All right, Mac. Cool it. Yes. You don't realise I am cool now. Dead cool. I'm not going to rush out and bash her head in. I'm not going to do anything in a temper. You should understand I've had years to think of it. Years of heat. Years of boiling over. I don't any more. I'm cool now. Steady. I don't get mad any more when she tries to rile me. That's over, Mac. I'm cool now I know what I have to do to stop her.'

'But stop her in what, Jim? Why don't you

just go? Change your name. Shift right away. Start a new life.'

'I thought of that years ago, Mac. But the world isn't a big place. She'd chase me anywhere to carry on hitting me. It's her life now. You find it hard to understand that, but that's her. That's what she's like.'

'Look, Jim. I don't bloody well believe you! You've got a bug in your head and the only way to get rid of it is to—'

'A bug? Let me tell you what the bug is. Some time ago now, after the fourth affair and making gibes about them to me about the fine men they were, she started demanding more clothes, more money to buy them. I couldn't give her any more without defaulting on everything else. Mortgage—you know the range. Well it was a row that went on for some time and then she said she'd do it her way. Do you know what she did, Mac?'

'I don't know, Jim. I don't know. But—'

'You haven't heard what she did? Haven't you?'

'Look, Jim, I've heard gossip, rumours, that sort of thing, but I just don't take any notice of them. They're vicious. Spiteful.'

'As she is,' Jim said. 'As she bloody is. Vicious and spiteful. Well, as you've only heard what she did from gossipers, I'll put you in the picture. The picture the gossipers were right about, Mac. She's a whore. You know that, of course. You always did know that, didn't you?'

'Jim, I don't take account of gossip, I tell you! I—'

'What she did when I couldn't give her any money for new clothes was set herself up as a call-girl, from our own house. She put adverts in sex magazines. She had a poncey boyfriend take nude pictures of her to bring in the customers. High-class escort and pleasure person. And she comes back in the morning and chucks the money at me. Two hundred—three hundred pounds, all over me like snow—I'm not heated, Mac. Don't say it again. This was a long time ago, or it seems it. Afterwards I went numb. I didn't know what to do. I wouldn't answer the phone any more. Men were ringing up all times—'

'Look, have you seen a solicitor about this, Jim? Have you?'

'No. I know what they'd think. "Lie back and live on it, you bloody little worm." That's what they'd think, Mac. You know that. You probably think a bit like that yourself, don't you?'

'For God's sake, Jim! You must pull yourself out of this. You're mad thinking you could cure everything by—by doing what you said. Think for a moment. Be practical. From what you say men are ringing up all the time. Well, if she isn't there won't they start wondering what's happened to her?'

'Who'd say anything? She's a high-class

whore. She doesn't cater for Tom, Dick and Harry. The gentlemen she obliges don't talk about it openly, and they certainly wouldn't go to the police, would they? My boss, for instance—'

'Your boss? Franklyn?'

'You'll lose your jaw if you drop it any further, Mac. Oh yes, Franklyn. She made a special point of having him. Her expertise is humiliation to infinity. You really don't know Geraldine, Mac. You just never saw through her, did you?'

Julia showed up at last. I got up, left my drink and went through the crowd to meet her.

'You'll lose our table!' she said.

'Let it go. I'm glad you showed up, but I wish you'd been on time. I've been roasted over there. Come on. We'll go to Mike's bar. I can't stand any more of that man, and there's no other table left here.'

'Oh, if you must,' she said. 'But how did you get roasted? You were by yourself there, weren't you?'

'I couldn't get out of earshot without losing the table.'

'But now you've given it away!'

'I'm sorry. It had a bit of an effect on me. I couldn't stop listening, and didn't want to. I was just locked on to it. They didn't think anybody could hear, either of them.'

We walked towards Mike's.

'Well, what were they talking about?'

'A man was talking about murdering his wife, and the other chap was trying to talk him out of it.'

'You should have found that enthralling, professionally.'

'I'm not a policeman, Julia. And in any case, the man needed a psychiatrist to listen, not me.'

'I think they like to be called something else now,' she said.

'Who? Murderers?'

'No. Psychiatrists.'

'I hadn't heard.'

'You will when you see one.'

'Julia, you are a clunk.'

'Coming from you, dear Mr Keyes, that's a compliment.'

'I thought this was to be a business lunch, not a courtship, Julia.'

'Were you gruesome before you overheard this terrible talk?'

'I'm always gruesome on Thursday, Julia.'

'Why Thursdays?'

'I don't like thunder. What would you like for an aperitif?' We sat down. The waiter was coming to us carrying a trayful of empty glasses through the crowd.

'Back in a minute,' he called as he went by. 'Menu's on the floor down there. See it?'

'Don't complain!' Julia said, holding up a hand and diving the other down below the table. 'I'll get it!' She bent down out of sight below the table, then straightened.

'What happened to the Age of Elegance?' I said. 'Groping around amongst the spit and sawdust for the menu—! Let's go to Jack's.'

'Sit down and shut up. I'm hungry, and I have to be back at half two.'

'If you'd been on time, we should have been able to—'

'If I'd been on time you wouldn't have heard that little man burning your ears off, so don't complain. Now let's see what we've got here—'

I watched her reading the menu with some pleasure. She was very beautiful. I have a weak strain of believing that all women are beautiful in one way or another. It is perhaps the reason why I have made so many errors in my life.

For a brief moment I wondered what sort of beautiful woman Jim's wife could be, if she had been able to make a call-girl career at thirty-four . . .

'I don't want any epicurean criticism,' Julia said. 'I'm going to have a Vienna steak with french fried.'

'The French culinary word for french fried is *Chips*,' I said with fine emphasis, 'and that for Vienna steak is junk.'

'I like junk,' she said, smiling very sweetly. 'That's why we do business.'

2

'Julia? Yes. I know I've only just seen you, but that was business. Would you like dinner tonight? Somewhere good. Soup and fish. Age of Elegance stuff. No—not tails. I was thinking half way there. Yes, I'm old-fashioned. I'll collect you. Seven? Early. But why not? We might do the theatre. Right. I'll be there.'

I looked up. My secretary was looking in, holding the door with one hand, a file in the other.

'What now, Monica?' I said.

'You are flippant. Something's worrying you.'

'What worries me is how women can form opinions on too little evidence. Is it possible to get a list of call-girl advertisers?'

'You must be worried if you feel that deprived.' She came in and the door closed itself. 'But if you feel really strained, I can spare an evening.'

'You're fired,' I said. 'Now, is it possible?'

'It means getting a collection of sex magazines. Who shall we send out to buy them?' She smiled.

'Suppose I said this inquiry had to do with murder?'

'I wouldn't believe you, because if it were murder, you'd be the first to call in the thin blue line.'

'Preventing a murder, perhaps?'

She cocked her head.

'What case is this? One of ours?'

'It hasn't happened,' I said. 'But it might. I think I have overheard the preliminary arrangements for the deed.'

'Seriously?'

'Yes.'

'Well, I'll go. I know Susie at the newsagents. I'll tell her you're feeling flat and need a few girlie pictures for the afternoon.'

'I don't care what you tell her,' I said. 'She thinks I'm sexless.'

'What!' She stared in real surprise.

'And when you get them, all I want are the ads and the phone numbers.'

'Then I needn't buy any, need I? Susie will let me take the numbers in her back room.'

'If she does, buy her a large box of her own chocolates. Say it's from me, but I'm shy.'

'I will not.'

During the afternoon I thought about the overheard talk almost constantly. I got to a pitch where I began arguing with myself that the men had been rehearsing a play, a film, a TV serial, but the sounds had been too real.

I used the electric portable in my office and wrote down as nearly as I could remember what they had said. I don't think I had it a lot wrong.

Writing it down helped to convince me even more that the murder would happen, and it would be very simple.

One way had been offered. The woman customarily answered the door at night with a hatchet in her hand. Jim had only to ring the doorbell one night—when she had no business appointment—and she would answer, with the hatchet. When she saw it was him, she could turn away and put the hatchet back on the table. Then he could pick it up, smash her skull in, drop the hatchet on the floor and go out again to some prepared alibi.

Given the unruly state of the neighbourhood at night he had described, he could be on a clear run.

Or he might not.

An amateur starting on a murder doesn't look on the scene from the police point of view. He looks at the whole scene as being what the police will see. He looks for clues in that whole scene.

The police worked the other way. They looked at the pieces of the jigsaw which would make up the picture. They built up the scene from small observed details and made a picture rather different from the one the murderer had made up for them.

He would be questioned, tripped and caught. Then he would be shut up for many years until he was old and broken and wasted.

Like Mac, I could not believe there was not another way out of it. Why couldn't he disappear? Why on earth should she follow him? Was her obsession about his humiliation so strong it would lead her anywhere?

Or was it that he, in his heart, could not leave her?

Could he be in such a state that he must keep her to him, even if it meant killing her to do it?

The idea of him keeping her dead body in a cupboard somewhere about the house turned my stomach, but it was a fact that some people did do such things. And it might not be a weird attachment that drove them, but an absorbing hatred and constantly needing a proof of triumph, by the sure knowledge that she was dead and he had decreed it and carried it out no matter how she had fought.

I was getting morbid.

At four, Monica came back with a list of names and numbers.

'It would be a suburban one,' I said. 'Try it on the computer.'

'Is there enough information here for it?' she said.

'Ask it.'

She went and asked it. It returned an answer of twenty-two suburban numbers and the addresses of those numbers.

'It's a lot,' she said.

'Yes. I should have thought it might get closer. Never mind. Thanks, dear.'

'Have you had your tea?'

'No. I won't bother now, thanks.'

She stared at the desk.

'You've been typing,' she said.

'Yes. One or two things I wanted to remember.'

'What am I here for?'

'To look beautiful and make me happy. Where are my letters?'

'I'll bring them in,' she said.

I signed the letters and left the office at five. The bar was open again. This time I went to the bar itself. The chief barman was there alone.

'You didn't stay for lunch this morning, Mr Keyes?'

'No. Something occurred. I'll have a gin and tonic—no; ginger beer and gin. I have a thirst. You saw me this morning?'

'Yes, sir.' He looked away and smiled at two other customers, in for a quick swallow before their trains left.

'Did you notice the two men in the end cubicle?'

'I did. The stranger was losing Scotch at a giant rate. Is that what you mean?'

'Do you know them?'

'I know Mr Maclean—' he stopped pouring for an instant as the ginger beer rose in froth, '—but the other man was a stranger. I don't remember seeing him before.'

'You know Mr Maclean?'

'Oh yes. He owns the printing works down Swan Alley, almost back of here. You know,

15

they do letterheads, cards, specialities, advertising pamphlets. James Maclean and Company. He's often in. Brings customers for lunch sometimes. Thank you, sir. Excuse me.'

He went to the other customers and I saw him press a bell under the counter as he noticed more hasty swallowers come in at the door. Two barmaids appeared in answer to the bell. They looked nice enough to brighten up the tired businessmen as they gazed at beauty through the bubbling bottoms of gins and tonics.

James Maclean and Company would be closed by then.

The work of the investigator needs infinite patience where human instinct is to rush in at once. James Maclean would have to wait.

I looked through the evening paper, my mind foolishly ranging over unprinted headlines like:

BLOODY MURDER IN HAMPSTEAD
───────
Police hunt Mad Axeman!

The thing was getting my mind into a bad area, yet I had heard only some tortured man saying he would do what he probably never would do. Saying and doing are different things. There are few people so determined that they do exactly what they've said they'd do.

I finished my drink and left. It was a fine evening in early spring so I walked the two miles back to my mews cottage.

As I was putting my key in the door a woman came up to me.

'Mr Keyes?' she said.

She had a charming, smiling sort of voice. I turned, admitted the identity and looked at her.

I am easily persuaded by beauty and she certainly had a lot of it. She was dark, with green eyes that looked as if they might laugh suddenly. She was fairly tall, with beautiful legs and figure rather disguised in a chinchilla coat.

She said, 'Your office told me you had left. When I told them it was important and personal, they said I might call.'

'They gave you my address?' I said, making a note to show anger in the morning.

'No. I had your address.' She smiled again.

I opened the door. 'Come in, Mrs—'

'Harrison,' she said.

She went in. When we were in the living-room she turned to me, her coat swinging open. She had an excellent figure.

'Mr Keyes, I am sorry to butt in on you, but, you see, it is a very urgent matter.'

'You said it was personal,' I said shortly.

'It is. I am sure my husband is planning to kill me.'

I wondered how many people the head barman did talk to about his customers.

CHAPTER TWO

1

I looked at the woman carefully. She was quite lovely to look at, and I guessed about thirty years old. Her attitude was one of quiet appeal with a sense of strain in the soft tone of her voice.

To me, the situation was quite incredible. It could not possibly be coincidence that I should have heard a husband threaten his wife in the morning, and to hear a wife saying she was threatened in the evening.

There had to be some connection through the bar where I had been, and by way of the informative head barman. He knew me and he knew the printing man.

'Will you help me, Mr Keyes?' she said.

'If you really believe your husband means such a dreadful thing, Mrs Harrison, you should go to the police,' I said. 'They will be able to help you.'

'There is a personal reason why I can't do that,' she said, and turned away for a second or two before she went on; 'I had hoped you would be able to help without my making this matter public.'

Initial shock was changing into curiosity in my head. It is a fatal weakness in my work to want to know more, specially if it is obviously better to have nothing to do with it.

'May I sit down? My shoes hurt.'

'Of course. Please be comfortable.' I decided to be polite and kind before I refused the help she wanted. The pause given by letting her rest her feet might also give her time to tell me more without my making any commitment.

She sat down and took one shoe off. There was something odd about that. Somehow I felt that if she really were in fear of her life she shouldn't be making a fuss about a sore foot.

It made me wonder if she was worried enough. After all it was her proposed murder she was talking about.

'I suppose it's hard to believe me,' she said, as quietly as before.

'Mrs Harrison, many men might threaten to murder their wives when they're in a rage. With some it's a figure of speech.'

'But a wife can tell the difference between that and a real threat,' she said.

'I suppose so.'

'You want to refuse me without hearing what I have to say.' Her voice never rose. There was not even reproach in it. Just a deep sadness.

'No, Mrs Harrison. No. But if what you

say is true, and you know your husband intends this dreadful thing, your only course is to go to the police. Surely you realise that?'

'I've told you; there is a personal reason why I can't.'

I sat on the arm of a chair facing her.

'But, Mrs Harrison, you should realise that if you really want help you'll have to say what that reason is anyway. The police, I assure you, are very discreet when it comes to people in real difficulty.'

She sighed.

'I'm sorry, Mr Keyes, but, you see, it would involve others to tell.'

'But do these others know that you are in danger? Wouldn't they agree to help if you needed it?'

'I can't presume upon goodwill, Mr Keyes.'

Her quietness had a sound of hopelessness about it that was very difficult to withstand.

'If you told me something about this whole thing I might be able to tell you how to get discreet help, but you must appreciate that firms like ours do not provide protection. That's something only the police can give.'

'Against one's husband?'

I saw the point, which in my determination not to be directly involved I had rather made light of.

'Has your husband been violent towards you?'

'Not physically. No.'

'Mentally?'

'Constantly.'

She scored with that one word. She was very beautiful and in distress. I tried not to look at her too much.

'How long have you been married, Mrs Harrison?'

'Twelve years.'

I was surprised. Twelve years was a damned long time to take to find out that the husband you're living with is a bad lot; so bad, you believe he would murder you.

'And recently you've had a good many rows?'

'No.' She shook her head and her voice was a little sharper. 'Oh no. He doesn't make rows. Perhaps he would feel better if he did. He sulks, but won't say what's the matter. He broods a lot, and I feel it's something I've done, but he won't say and I can't guess what it is. It begins to give one the feeling of being watched, spied on, even though he isn't there.'

'Yes, I can understand the feeling,' I said. 'And his attitude has continued like that?'

'Yes.'

'For how long?'

'I don't know for certain. I suppose it must be about two years.'

'Getting worse?'

'No. More on a continuous level. Water

dripping on a stone. Or as the Chinese do it, on somebody's forehead.'

'And this has gone on for two years?'

'I should say about that. Yes.'

'And for the ten years before that? Were relations better then?'

'He is intensely jealous. About two years after we married an old boyfriend of mine called on business, and for weeks after that he was sullen; he watched everything I did; he listened in on my phone calls. Everything. It was awful.'

'You have an extension phone?'

'Yes.'

'Where do you live, Mrs Harrison?'

'Hampton Court. Close by the Park.'

That was not the sort of place I had imagined Jim to live in. His picture of marauding muggers, and violent knockers-on-doors was more the scene of a declining city outskirt than Hampton Court.

'A house or a flat?'

'A house. It was my mother's. She left it to me when she died, about ten years ago.'

'And you live there with your husband?'

'Yes. Just the two of us. It is quite a small house by Regency standards.'

Regency standards in Hampton Court didn't match up at all with the picture of the prostitute wife waiting for muggers with a chopper.

I must have made a mistake and the matter

was after all a coincidence.

But then I felt uneasy. It was such a colossal coincidence. Such a huge freak of chance that I should have heard a husband in the morning and the wife at night, both talking of murder, yet both total strangers. Both talking of the husband planning to murder the wife, yet the descriptions of the neighbourhoods seeming quite different.

But the head barman could have managed these things. I used that bar quite often for lunch, and when I came to think of it, he had sent us a client once before, and one we had been able to help.

'Mrs Harrison,' I said, 'from what you've said so far I find it hard to believe that you feel threatened physically. What happened to make you so sure you were in danger?'

Curiosity and interest in her was leading me by the nose to disaster, but I realised it then and tightened the reins on my impetuosity.

'I was told by a friend of his, who was very worried about it.'

A friend. The friend at the table with him. Mac, the friend who had listened and tried to persuade the madman away from his bloody intention.

But if the friend had told her, then he had probably more interest in her than in the murderous husband.

'A friend told you? Did he advise you to

leave your husband?'

'Yes, but I can't do that for no reason, and you forget, the house is mine. I wouldn't leave that for him to move some popsy into as soon as I'd gone.'

'Do you think he might do that?'

'He has quite a selection. Men jealous of their wives usually do have some relief hanging around somewhere, don't they?' She cocked her head.

She seemed more at ease than at first, but there was still that line in her brow, that quickness in her eye which betrayed strain and, perhaps, fear.

'Is there another woman?'

'It would be the first time for years if there isn't.'

She knew he had other women while he stayed being jealous of his wife. He's potty, I thought.

That made the story and possibility of violence much more reasonable to suppose.

'What sort of man is he?'

'Far too imaginative. I think that's what makes him sullen and morose. He gets an idea in his head, expands it, decorates it and paints it in bloody colours, then he broods on it. It's a kind of self-torture, but it has always disturbed me because one can never tell just when he might pass the point when he can't stand it any more.'

'Then he could be violent?'

'I'm sure he could. You know, people who hold themselves back for a long time can explode.'

For some reason that sentence held me back from making too much of this story. It was odd. To me it had a kind of pantomime effect on my imagination. I visualised the man bursting from rage.

And there was something else that I could not quite imagine in detail.

How had the friend told her about the threat to her life? To be able to make such a warning to somebody else's wife seems to imply a very close relationship in the first place. An ordinary friendly acquaintance could not call and say, 'Mrs Harrison, I think you ought to know your husband plans to murder you.'

He would be rejected by the lady as a fool, a liar, a mischief-maker or a certifiable lunatic.

No, I felt the man had to be close so that she would give proper thought to what he had to say.

'You have thought about this possibility a great deal, I imagine?'

'Well, yes! Of course I have!' She was surprised.

'And have you thought how you might protect yourself against this threat? I mean, if it really did happen, how do you imagine it happening? Violently? Or by some trick, or by interfering with food?'

'I have thought of it, but I can't quite imagine it happening—or how it might happen—' She broke off and looked a little lost.

'But you think really that if anything did happen it would be violent?'

'I feel it would be. Yes.' She shuddered suddenly and looked away. 'I'm sorry.'

'I must repeat, Mrs Harrison, you must talk to the police about this—' Then I realised that I had overlooked a possibility, but did not think it was a very sensible one. 'Have you spoken to your solicitor?'

'Of course not! He acts for both of us. And I certainly wouldn't go to a strange one. If it had to be put to a desperate choice, I would rather choose the police.'

'And that you refuse to do. But why, then, risk coming to me?'

'Because if I saw you unofficially and you refused to help, this wouldn't go down on the record,' she said, frankly.

'I see,' I said.

That look of frankness was so clear and perfect that I had the thought I might be dealing with a consummate actress.

'Tell me something,' I said suddenly.

'Of course.'

'Have you a hatchet in the house for splitting firewood?'

'There is one, yes, but it's not used for

anything. There was a firemen's strike, years ago, and my husband volunteered to run the switchboard for emergencies. He actually was never wanted, but they gave him this fireman's axe as a memento.'

Oh dear, I thought.

2

There was no longer any doubt in my mind that this was the lady whose husband had threatened to murder her in his conversation that morning. That his friend had tried so hard to dissuade him made the closeness of his friendship plain.

The friend, Mac, had not spoken of the intended victim as also a close friend, but I had no doubt that he went straight and told her to be on the defensive, and that he did it because of their closeness.

The fact that the lady had called proved, as far as I was concerned, that the warning had been made by Mac.

As they had sat together, Jim had had his back to me, which is why I had heard so clearly, not above, but more in front of, the noise in the bar.

Mac, on the other hand, had only to look past Jim's head to see me, and he had known who I was from the barman.

Thus the whole link was clear in my mind, and the wife's ploy of ringing the office and pretending the call was on a personal matter had clicked.

The reason why it had may have been that, due to my uncertain life until then, there were ladies who had rung up from time to time wishing to see me, and my secretary had clearly thought this call one of those.

'If you feel you can't help me yourself, Mr Keyes, could you tell me what I ought to do? Bearing in mind what I have told you.'

'Mrs Harrison, if there is a reason why you can't be open, I don't see how anybody could help. I mean, if you could trust the integrity of the police and went to them, they would want to know where they stood, and why you wouldn't go to them in the first place.'

'And so would anybody else, you seem to imply.'

'Of course. Supposing, for a moment, a professional man took up your case, if he didn't know the whole truth about it he might find himself on the wrong side of the law.'

She thought a moment.

'Yes. I understand what you mean, Mr Keyes. But, bearing in mind that difficulty which is a constraint, can you think of no way I could get help?'

'I need time to think about it, Mrs Harrison. Something may occur to me, but with this difficulty it isn't very likely. In the meantime I suggest you don't go back to the house tonight. Ring up your husband. Make an excuse and find a hotel.'

'As you suggest that, you believe what I have said,' she said, putting on her shoe. 'That in itself is a help, Mr Keyes.' She stood up and held out her hand. 'Thank you so much for listening and being so kind.'

'I'm sorry I really can't help more directly, but you do understand?'

She was very beautiful and I was sorry.

'May I call you tomorrow?' she said. 'Here?'

'Yes. I may have thought of something, but I can't promise. You do understand?'

'Yes. Thank you again. Goodbye.'

As I closed the door behind her I felt really sorry I couldn't help. She was so beautiful it could have been a pleasure.

I went back into my living-room and poured a dry sherry. As I sipped it I thought again about the one thing she could not mention in the affair.

She was a call-girl? Was that it?

As I went upstairs to shower and change, glass in hand, I realised that, reminding myself of that fact about her meant I was close to believing the whole lot of what I had overheard and what she had told me.

There were so many parallel details and the axe seemed to lock the two stories together.

Of course, no two people tell the truth about the same event. There are always differences of stress, of vision and of personal bias. It is a sad fact of witnesses. Four witnesses about the same incident will give different versions of it, and one must pick out the mean, the average, of the lot to get the truth.

'You look so happy I think you must have had a foot run over by a steamroller,' Julia said and kissed me lightly.

'I'm sorry. It must have been a passing thoughtful mood. Seeing you has improved the outlook.'

At the end of dinner at the Savoy, I told her.

'This morning I told you I'd overheard a man talking of killing his wife,' I said. 'When I got home this evening a woman was there claiming her husband was planning to kill her.'

She looked at me with an amused, cocked-head smile.

'Somebody is pulling your little leg,' she said.

'It couldn't have been arranged,' I said. 'I overheard the man.'

'Were you meant to?'

'Have you been to The Raven before?'

'In the hip-bath cubicles? Yes. I had lunch with you two or three months back. The food was good, I thought. I'm flattered you don't remember. I don't know why I accept your invitations.'

'They've altered the back wall since you came,' I said. 'It must reflect sound. I heard the man clearly, but he spoke very quietly most of the time. It was embarrassing.'

'But it was fascinating,' she said.

'He said he would kill her with an axe.'

'Well?'

'The woman who called said they had a presentation axe in the house.'

'Funny present. But outsider, me, doesn't really get such a shock from it as you do. A lot of households must have axes for cutting firewood, making logs fit the fireplace and for cutting up joints into chops.'

'It's not a cleaver. It's a fireman's axe, the lady said.'

'Well, it couldn't cut chops but it can chop firewood, and anybody who got in the way, I suppose. But, seriously; yes, it is odd, but do you really think it serious?'

'I don't know. I feel it is.'

'Deep down?'

'Well—yes. Yes, I do.'

'Well if you feel like that, sweetie, you'll have to do something, because if it did happen you'd feel horrible.' She looked at me calmly. 'Did you refuse the lady?'

'No. I said I would have to think. I told her to find a hotel for the night.'

'Very wise. But what about all the other nights? Or do you think this murderous husband will forget it all tomorrow?' She looked earnest. 'She'll have to go for good.'

'She won't. The house is hers.'

'Oh, I see her problem. Or do you think that might be the husband's idea? To scare her off for good?'

I thought about it.

'I hadn't thought of it that way,' I confessed.

'You see the men were together, almost in your ear. The friend listens, having put them both where you will hear them. You get the m26message. The friend tells the wife, and tells her about you. She comes to you. Hey *voilà!*'

'It's a thought,' I said. 'But it's too much of a long shot.'

'But it's a long shot anyway, isn't it? As far as coincidence can go, this is about as far as I've ever heard one go.'

'Agreed. But it's happened.'

'It's happened to you. You don't actually know this Mac fellow, do you?'

'No. But I think he knew who I was. The barman there is a beer-spilling who's who.'

'My idea really bases on whether the printer knew who you were before or after this morning.'

'And how do we find that out? By asking the barman? If I did he'd start wondering and once he starts wondering he'll ask Mac questions and Mac will guess what he's fishing for. Then we shall all be suspicious of each other and nobody will be forthcoming about anything.'

'And there is this other small point,' she

said, laying a hand on mine across the table. 'Does it really matter to you?'

Again she cocked her head very prettily.

'It may seem odd, my dear, but though to an outsider this might look contrived, and so like some kind of hoax, I heard the man and I met the woman, and both were very deeply frightened of what might happen.'

'You think the man was frightened, too?'

'Of himself. Yes.'

'So it's really got you. Well, if it's got that effect on a hardened old professional like you, then I ought to help as much as I can.'

'You are very sweet, Julia.'

I took her back to her flat later and we sat over a pot of Darjeeling tea and listened to Chopin. It was so pleasant the War of the Harrisons withdrew to the back of my mind.

At quarter to twelve, I left and drove back to the mews cottage. The phone was ringing as I opened the door. I suppose the earlier events of the day caused me to feel a small uneasiness as I lifted the receiver.

'Mr Keyes?'

It was a man's voice and unfamiliar. I admitted the name. He went on almost in a gabble.

'You don't know me, but I am in need of your help, Mr Keyes. I am in the most serious trouble, I assure you, and . . .'

'Who are you?'

The interruption seemed to stun him. He

replied after a break of several seconds.

'My name is Harrison. We don't know each other, but I have been recommended to you . . .'

'You said you were in serious trouble, Mr Harrison. If that's the case, the people to go to are the police.'

'I can't go to them,' he said quickly.

'Why not?'

'Because it wouldn't be help they would give me. If I went to them now, the only help I would get would be through the cell bars!'

Mixed ideas flew through my head, of hoaxes, lunatics and dipsomaniacs.

'In that case, Mr Harrison, I can't help you. Good night!'

I felt that if he had gone on he would say he had just murdered his wife. That would cap the whole day's events and prove it to be some elaborate hoax without any purpose but to make an idiot out of me.

But why?

There was always some damned question likely to spoil a night's rest.

I didn't get one in any case, because at one forty-five the front door bell rang more than once and without giving interval enough for me to get up.

CHAPTER THREE

1

The door bell must have rung five times while I switched on the light, got up, slung on a dressing-gown, stepped into slippers and went downstairs to answer it.

I can't say now if I had been awakened from a bad dream, but at the door I hesitated and, contrary to usual practice, shouted through the panels.

'Who is it?'

I heard the voice faintly. It was weak with despair and the thickness of the door made it sound almost like a whisper.

'Mr Keyes! Please . . . ! Let me in, please . . .'

Mrs Harrison was back. I unfastened the door and opened it. She almost fell in, regained her balance and stood back against the hall wall.

'Shut it—quickly! Please!'

I closed the door.

'What on earth's happened?' I said. 'Didn't you find a hotel?'

'Yes, I—'

I thought she would pass out, and took hold of her. I led her into the room and made her sit down.

'Take it easy for a moment. I'll get you a

drink.'

I poured her a brandy and gave it to her. She sat there with the glass in her hand and just stared at it. She looked to be in a bad state of shock.

'Drink it,' I said.

She pulled herself together and drank the brandy in a gulp. She began to choke slightly, as if she had taken herself by surprise in drinking so much.

'You'll feel better in a moment.'

I watched her carefully. Her clothes were not as smart as when she had called before. They looked as if she had slung them on in a hurry.

I went to the window, lifted the curtain at one side and looked out. The mews looked empty, but there are nooks and crannies in such old places and one can never be quite sure of emptiness in them.

'Is he out there?' she said in a frightened whisper.

'Your husband?'

'Yes. Is he?'

'I can't see anyone out there. Do you mean that your husband followed you here?'

She put a hand to her forehead.

'I don't know—I'm not sure—Somebody—'

I left her silent for a minute or more. I was not at all sure she had not been physically hit as well as mentally, she was in such a state.

'Tell me about the hotel,' I said.

'I went to one near here. They knew me, but they would not—'

'Go on.'

'They would not let me in. They said they were full, but they weren't. I went to another. They knew me there, too. But they were the same. They wouldn't have me—'

She was greatly distressed about that, apart from anything else. I sat down opposite her. In my mind the story about the call-girl came back and it was possible a hotel might refuse a single woman whom they knew to have been there before as a whore.

I did not press that point, and I did not realise at the time I left it unpressed because somewhere in my mind I was taking the wretched husband's story for the truth.

'Could your husband have guessed you would go to one of those hotels?'

'Yes. I believe he could. He knows where I have been before. We have stayed together at several hotels at different times. He was forcing me to go home—!'

She stopped there and became quite still, staring through me to something at a great distance away.

'Did you go home?' I said.

She didn't answer for some time, but sat staring at that faraway scene in her mind.

'Yes.' She unfroze and looked up at me for a moment. 'Yes. I went home.'

I went back to the sideboard and poured a beer. I was very dry in the throat, as if the woman's tension was being broadcast about the room. I could almost feel her fear and yet she was so uncannily quiet about it.

As I asked no question, she went on after a minute or more.

'The house was empty when I got there. Somehow I was sure it would be. I had a weird feeling that he had been following me that night, and getting me refused each place I went.

'I went into the house, shut the door, bolted and put the chain on it. I made sure the back door was fastened the same way and the alarm was on. The burglar alarm. It's on all the windows and doors. Then I sat down and waited . . .'

'You waited for him to come back?'

'Yes. I just sat and waited. I knew he would come.'

'Go on, please.'

'The grandmother clock struck. It gave me a fearful shock. I was that tensed up. Although I knew he would not get in without the burglar alarm going off, because the chains and bolts were on the doors—'

I waited a few seconds.

'What time was it?' I said, hoping to start her off again.

'Eleven. Yes. It was eleven. I went out into the hall and looked and checked the door again, in case he had got in somehow when the clock was striking—'

'How could he have got in?'

'No. Of course, he couldn't. I went back into the kitchen and sat down, and listened ... and listened ... I listened till I could hear things all over the house; creaks, little cracking, water shifting in the pipes—It seemed as if there were little sounds everywhere, little sounds, like somebody creeping along the carpet upstairs—'

She stopped and this time dropped her head into her hands as if about to weep. I felt intense sorrow for her. It is one thing to be attacked physically. There is the chance of avoiding it, or by defence, but there is no defence against the attack by fear from within oneself.

She raised her head defiantly and went on.

'At first I thought—as you're probably thinking now—that I was just going mad, but I'm not an abnormally nervous person, Mr Keyes, whatever you think at this moment.

'It was because I knew that, I began to question my imagination, and I listened more intently. I went out into the hall and opened the clock and stopped it with my hand so that I could listen acutely.

'I heard somebody move somewhere upstairs. I knew that then, and I know it now. I let the clock go again. I don't think I had strength to hold the pendulum any more.

The clock started to clack about and whirr, and I was so desperate to be able to listen, I swung the pendulum again to make the ticking regular. It was easier to hear like that. I didn't know any other way to keep a clock from making weird sounds except by making it go. One gets used to the rhythm, and it's easier to hear—I *had* to hear, you see.

'I went up the stairs very slowly. All the doors to the rooms were wide open. They never were normally. It made me feel I was being watched from several directions at once.

'Listening again got difficult because of my heart starting to thump. I stood there near the top of the stairs, dead still, trying to quieten it down. I could feel waves of cold running right down through my body so my legs felt weak. I hung on to the stair rail, tightly, so I shouldn't let go altogether and fall down the stairs.

'I was by then terrified, Mr Keyes. I controlled that first wave of panic, but the horror of the situation was quite beyond my control and, I believe, anybody else's.

'You see, for that last few minutes I was slowly realising that my care in locking up the house to keep my husband out had been completely useless.

'The truth was, I had locked him in with me.'

I was beginning to feel the awful strains she

must have gone through in that dreadful house.

'Did you see him?'

'No. But he has that kind of creepy mind, like the child who hides and watches then gives himself away by sniggering. My husband can control his sniggering. He has played games on me like that before, only tonight there was no game.

'I went downstairs, trying to look as if I acted normally. As if I were satisfied nobody was up there. So he would think I wasn't on my guard.

'I wanted him to show himself. I felt if he did, I wouldn't feel so bad. I would be frightened, but not terror-stricken. If I could see him, I might be able to defend myself.

'Then, as I came down into the hall again, I saw the axe was missing. I think that put the cap on it. I think my heart stopped altogether, and I hung on to the stair rail and tried to listen again. Listen for the sound of someone creeping—But then I realised that anyone creeping would be coming behind me, and I turned round and looked everywhere I could.

'All the doors were open down there too, all but the kitchen door, which is a swinger and closes itself—'

She stopped. I gave her some seconds' pause.

'Was the axe kept in the hall?'

'My husband kept it there. It was in a leather sort of holster. It hangs on the wall. It did, until tonight.'

'I see. What did you do then?'

'I shouted to him to come down. I shouted and shouted. There was no answer. Then I realised I was being a fool. I was showing him I was frightened, which is what he always wants. Only this time, I was quite sure that he wanted more than that . . .'

She got up and stood for a moment looking at the carpet. Then she went on:

'I pulled myself together, and went out into the kitchen. I had to get out of the house so he could not follow. I decided to leave by the back door, go to the garage at the bottom of the garden and take the car. You were the only person I could think of who could help me. I locked the back door on the outside and ran down the garden. As I opened the garage door I looked back. There are street lights by the river path. They shine on the back door. I saw the door opening . . .

'I went into the garage and locked the door. I opened the main doors and got in the car. His motor-bike was there beside it. I did not know how to damage it to stop him using it, so when I backed out I turned the wheel so the car smashed into it and knocked it over.

'I drove very fast, but after only a few minutes a motor-bike started coming up behind me. I didn't know what to do. I watched it in the mirror. It was coming up fast as if it would overtake me, but it didn't. It stayed there, right behind. I'd been near to screaming all that night, but I let it go then. I don't know if anybody heard. I was just hanging on the wheel trying to steer along a road that was narrower than I could steer—

'I slowed down and turned off, and kept turning and turning until I was lost, but that bloody bike stayed right behind. Sometimes I lost it, but it always came back.

'Then suddenly it passed me and tried to draw across. I just went ahead and hit it. What then happened I don't know. I got out and left the car on the pavement with the bike underneath. I ran. As I turned the corner of the street I looked back.

'He was getting up from the wreck and starting to run after me. He is still running after me, but he's limping now—Oh God! What can I do?'

She began to cry then. It prevented me from giving the advice I had given before: that she must go to the police. Instead, I let her cry her anguish down several points until she was calm once more.

2

'I'll get some tea,' I said. 'That will do you good.' I was going to get her into a frame of mind where she would see sense in my advice.

'Let me come with you!' she said at once. 'I don't want to be alone.'

'Come,' I said, there being nothing else I could think of.

She sat at the table. I made the tea.

'You say that the clock struck eleven after you'd got into the house? How long after?'

'I wasn't in much of a mood to know . . . oh, perhaps twenty minutes, say—Oh! The clock! It had been losing time. There was a man coming to set it properly. It could have been slow.'

'Very?'

'Perhaps a quarter of an hour. No. It couldn't have been as much as that—No, wait! Wait! It must have been *twelve* it struck.'

I saw she was staring at a clock on the cooker which then pointed at twenty-five to two.

'Yes. Twelve. Because I went upstairs and listened, then came downstairs, and didn't know what to do—then I saw the axe gone—I didn't run then, you see. I shouted. I thought he might come down—then I walked into the kitchen. I tried to look as if I didn't care—wasn't frightened. Yes. It must have been twelve the clock struck. I counted wrong. Or perhaps I didn't really count at all. I can't remember.'

'At about midnight a man rang up here,' I said. 'He told me he was Mr Harrison, and that he was in serious trouble and needed help before the police found him.'

I watched her very carefully then.

'At about twelve?' she said. 'But that couldn't have been Jim! He was in the house. I would have heard the phone!'

'You said there was a line in the house?'

'Did I? Yes, there is one. In the bedroom. But the door was open. I would have heard him.'

'Mrs Harrison, you must admit there is something very odd about this. You come to me in trouble and say you can't go to the police because of another matter. Then a Mr Harrison rings up in great trouble and needs help, but can't go to the police.'

She was shocked. She stared at me as if she didn't believe what I'd said.

'*No!*' she said.

'Is there something your husband feels guilty from, something done before tonight?'

She seemed flabbergasted and then shook her head.

'There may be something,' she said. 'I don't know. We've not been close. Perhaps I didn't make that clear. We have been living our own lives—'

I gave her tea.

'What does your husband do, Mrs Harrison?'

'He is a dealer in antique jewellery.'

'Is he successful?'

'Sometimes and sometimes not. It's a sharp world, Mr Keyes. My husband is not the sharpest of men.'

I went to the window, took the curtain aside and looked out along the little walled garden. I was not looking for anybody, but just avoiding looking at her too often, because by then I was aware she had a way of attracting me to her view, although it was not obvious when she was doing it.

'Have you a career, Mrs Harrison?' I turned back then.

'I have an interest in a meal service. Girls go out and provide dinners for private parties. You know the sort of thing.'

'It keeps you busy?'

'Like all such things, business varies.' She sounded impatient then.

I went back to the table, poured more tea and sat facing her.

'Right; let me go over things again. Your husband confides to James Maclean that he feels like murdering you—'

Her eyes grew suddenly big.

'I never mentioned James Maclean!' she said.

I went on. 'And Mr Maclean, being a close friend of yours as well as of your husband, warns you.'

She was dumbstruck and her astonishment looked genuine.

'How do you know—?'

'You know my business, Mrs Harrison. That's why you came to me.'

'Did my husband say—?'

'You told me it couldn't have been your husband who rang me around midnight.'

'No. I was there. I would have heard—'

She leant her elbows on the table and covered her face with her hands.

'I'm dead-beat,' she said. 'I can't even think straight. What the hell am I going to do?'

'You could tell me the truth, Mrs Harrison,' I said quietly. 'That might help everybody.'

'The reason I can't is that it isn't mine to tell,' she said without uncovering her face entirely. 'It's shared, you see. Bloody well shared!' She dropped her hands then. 'And it holds me by the throat so I can't help myself even if I wanted to!'

Both she and her husband had this curious lock-off place in their calls for help. If one discarded coincidence, and there had been too much already for my liking, then the secret of both was shared by a common person.

This seemed to suggest that husband and wife were closer than they protested. Which went on to suggest they were in agreement with each other.

In which case it was out of the question that one would want to murder the other after so much advance publicity on the proposal.

I walked to the window again and looked out in order to try and sort my thoughts out on the subject of the proposed murder of Mrs Harrison.

My instinct all along had been to believe the woman, because her quiet distress had seemed so real to me.

And yet the husband's call had sounded genuine, because it had been disjointed. It had no sign of having been thought out beforehand, which fake phone calls mostly are.

Then it occurred to me that something quite extraordinary was in my mind, though I was not quite sure how it got there.

It was an idea that Harrison was scared he might murder his wife, but that the wife was a different woman from the one who was with me, fearing she would be murdered by her husband.

I made some more tea. She watched me. She was by then very tired, but still seemed to watch me as if I would suddenly pull the rabbit of solution out of my hat. But solution to what?

Then I realised an omission from the whole story of hers.

I had heard the husband saying why he would murder her, but she was always hidden behind this 'shared secret'.

I poured more tea, then sat down opposite her.

'Why does he want to murder you? Give me a straight motive without mentioning the name of any third person, Mrs Harrison.'

She did not reply.

'A motive, Mrs Harrison. Tell me why.'

'The motive is in his imaginings,' she said. 'All of it is right there in his head, building up, getting stronger every minute!'

That tied in with the picture of a murderous lunatic stalking her in the silence of the house, trying to terrify her, and then pursuing her on the motor-bike through the night streets—

But I hadn't seen any of that. It could all have been a product of *her* imagination. The whole thing; the terrible tension of the time in the house; the near panic of being pursued through the streets and the final desperate running from the scene of the wreck to—

My house?

Surely in such a state of sustained agony the nearest policeman would be the target of a demand for help.

Perhaps she hadn't seen one. Perhaps she had seen nobody at all but the man inevitably behind her as she ran.

It would have been very unusual to have seen nobody at all during a flight of that kind.

'Where did you hit the motor-bike?' I said.

'Just round the corner from here.'

'You were heading for my house anyhow?'

'You were the only person in the world I

could think of. I was desperate. Damn it! I still am! What the hell am I going to do? If I go out of here—'

She gave a little shrug of hopelessness and sat back in her chair, as if she had given up any fight that remained in her.

'Oh well—let him bloody come,' she said dully. 'Who cares?'

'I care,' I said. 'But to care a bit more I must know more. You've told me about the horrible events of the night, now tell me why your husband imagines dreadful things about you that he wants to punish you for them.'

'I don't know exactly what he imagines—'

'You know what fires his imaginings. What is it? Jealousy? Humiliation? Desperation or just plain hatred?'

'Jealousy. It's always jealousy.'

'Have you any lovers?'

'Well, that's a very direct question—'

'You have asked me for direct help, Mrs Harrison! Have you?'

'There was one, but not now.'

'Did your husband know?'

'I couldn't tell you that. He imagines I have dozens of lovers. He even accused me of being on the level of a call-girl.'

She said that very quietly, and I felt my guns spiked.

I heard a faint sound out in the passage. I could not think what it was, but recently a cat had been getting in through a loose fanlight over the back door.

Excusing myself I went to the kitchen door and looked out to the passage. It was empty. I listened and at the same time remembered the story of her listening in that house at Hampton Court. Being stalked by the unseen seemed at that moment to be a very real situation indeed.

I went along the passage and into the living-room. It was empty, yet somehow I had a feeling that it was not.

My liking for comfortable furniture gives many a hiding-place where lighter stuff would not. I even began to walk about looking behind big chairs and the sofa before my tension eased and I felt a tinge of foolishness.

Yet as I turned to go back I had a feeling of unfinished business and that the room was not as empty as it looked.

My front door was not bolted or chained. Locks can be picked—

And if the husband was really a homicidal lunatic, this was the sort of thing he would do; creep about, scaring a victim into defencelessness—

A sudden violent knocking began at the front door. I felt a momentary draining of blood from my head, making my face feel cold.

CHAPTER FOUR

1

I stood in the middle of the room, undecided. The knocking at the door should have cancelled the feeling that somebody had got into the house, but it didn't. I felt that here was somebody calling while the man was in the house. I felt the caller was interrupting an important search.

The knocking stopped. I looked carefully round the room again. There was only one standard lamp shining and it cast too many shadows behind the heavier furniture.

I went to the door to snap on the main lights, but as I did so, the knocking at the front door began again.

It sounded as if the caller imagined I was asleep and was determined to wake me up. The urgency of the noise made me go into the small hall and open the door.

A medium-sized man stood there. He was an agitated man. His face was dark with sunburn; his hair and bushy eyebrows were white as snow. His tie was loosened and his shirt collar open, as if he found the heat of the cool night too much.

'Mr Keyes? I'm sorry, but it is an urgent matter and I believe you are the only one who can help me!'

'Damn it! It's two o'clock in the morning!'

'It's about Mrs Harrison. My name is Franklyn.'

The name Franklyn rang a little bell in my mind. It was the name of Harrison's boss. The man himself had said so.

As I, protesting, let him into the hall and closed the door, I realised that he might be able to tell me something about the mystery woman and her husband. My position in this disjointed matter was that I had been involved, in spite of my not very gullible nature, and really wanted to know what the truth of the matter was.

I led Franklyn into the living-room and offered him a seat. He refused.

'I'm afraid that something serious has happened, but as it is not directly my affair, I thought I had better see you first as Mrs Harrison told me she had asked your help.'

'The police are there for this sort of problem, Mr Franklyn.'

'It might not be a police matter yet,' he said. 'Mr Harrison said he had picked up an important piece—I'm sorry. I'll explain. My firm deals in antiques of every description and Mr Harrison is my chief buyer for jewellery.'

He seemed to me to be slightly confused, and as I listened I sometimes managed a glance round the room, upon which the main lights now shone, but there were still places where a man might be hiding there.

And then I realised how absurd my thinking was. My house is not small—that is, the rooms aren't—but even so to imagine a man hiding around amongst the furniture was far-fetched.

At least, it became far-fetched when somebody else was in the room with me, though quite plausible when one was alone there.

'Mr Harrison had something of interest for you. Yes?' I prompted.

'He had asked me to call at once, even up to one this morning,' Franklyn said. 'I'm a late bird myself, Mr Keyes. I got to his house at a quarter to one. There was no answer. I knew from earlier visits that there had been trouble with the bells and when my knocking wasn't heard either, I went round to the back.'

'You usually call at the back if there's no answer at the front?'

'I am a regular caller. We don't normally have all the jewellery items at our offices, and Harrison has a very good safe.'

He took a hasty breath. He was very upset—or perhaps frightened—about something.

'The back door was open and the lights inside were all on, something which is not so easy to see from the front of the house, because of heavy curtains.

'I went in and called out, but no one

answered. I had a strong sense of something being wrong—' He paused as if uncertain of what to say next.

'What made you think something was wrong?' I said.

'There had been trouble between Harrison and his wife.'

'Did you know Mrs Harrison well?'

'Very well. I had intended to marry her when my divorce came through, but she married Harrison instead.'

And thus he provided himself with the start of a motive for getting his own back on the lady, if one should ever need it.

'Did your divorce come through?'

'Aren't we getting away from the point?'

'Did it?'

'No, it didn't. The lawyers were frightened about possibilities of collusion. But what has that—?'

'I'm trying to get a picture into which I could fit a picture of you calling at the back door at one in the morning. That isn't normal procedure, is it?'

'It's not unusual for us.'

'Very well. You reached the back door, which was open. Did you go in?'

'I went right in and called for Jim. I knew he couldn't be in bed because the door was open. Nobody answered. I went through into the hall. It had a fine floor of polished oak and there was a pool of blood by the bottom of the stairs.'

'Blood? Are you sure?'

'Quite. I touched it with my finger to make sure of the colour. There were one or two more spots going away towards the back door. Also a large Persian rug, which normally lies in that area, was missing altogether. It was a show piece that Mrs Harrison was very fond of.'

'You're suggesting somebody was hurt and was carried away on the rug?'

'It would slide over the polished floor fairly easily. Yes.'

'What did you do?'

'I went upstairs in case something really bad had happened and one of them was hurt up there, but the place was empty. I came down again and looked in the rooms, but nobody was there.'

'Did you notice anything missing, apart from the rug?'

'He had a presentation fireman's axe which normally hangs in the hall. That had gone but the holster was up there. I wouldn't have noticed the axe was missing if the holster hadn't been there still.'

'You noticed all these things but still didn't call the police?'

'Mr Keyes, Harrison has a very peculiar idea of a joke. On one occasion he got blood from a butcher and spilt it around the place, then left a chopper about and other things calculated to cause alarm. Somebody called the police in that time. Harrison was fined for wasting police time. They believed he'd called them in the first place.'

'Where did this happen?'

'In the garage at the bottom of his garden.'

'You saw all these signs in the house, but you thought it might be another hoax?'

'No. Quite honestly I did not think it would turn out to be another hoax. He had been hinting about killing his wife, and she was duly frightened of him.'

'Is he unbalanced?'

'No. It's just now and again a strange sort of violence shows up. He always makes out it's meant to be funny, but it just isn't.

'Anyhow, I made sure nobody was in the house and then went down the garden and looked in the garage. The car had gone, but his bike was there, and it looked as if the car had smashed into it because . . .'

'The bike was there?'

He looked surprised.

'I've just told you it was. And it was damaged.'

'Was it damaged too badly for him to ride it?'

He stared.

'Well, I don't know! If he had killed his wife he wouldn't take her away on a bike, would he?'

'No. But if she was running away he might

have followed on the bike after she took the car.'

'If she was running and he following, who was hurt and how and why was the rug missing?'

'Let us go back to the beginning, Mr Franklyn. When did you hear that his wife was frightened that he would murder her?'

'Late afternoon. She phoned me.'

'And said she was frightened her husband might try to kill her?'

'That's what she said.'

'Did you believe her?'

'I don't know.'

'But what did you do about it?'

'I told her it was another of his brainstorms. I said he'd been worried about business lately.'

'Why was he worried?'

'He had bought two pieces for us for quite a large sum, but one of them turned out to be an extremely clever fake. It was only found after all sorts of chemical and electrical tests and microscopic search. But for those tests any expert would have taken it for genuine.'

'But it worried him?'

'It shattered him. He went to pieces for several days. He had always prided himself on his expertise.'

'And when he was worried he was liable to make these extreme jokes, like putting pig's blood about?'

'Yes. It was at times of despair.'

'Would you say Mrs Harrison was a good wife to him?'

'I would say she stood a lot from him, but she is not a weak woman.'

'Did she give him cause for jealousy, so far as you know?'

'She did. That was one of his excuses for threatening her.'

'He had threatened her before?'

'Not with murder—to my knowledge, of course. But then naturally, I don't know he ever threatened her. I was not in a position to know for certain. He was a man who would utter some threat against someone not there, but fail to carry it out. I always thought he was just letting off steam at a safe distance.'

'Then why should this latest threat have worried you?'

'Because *she* told me. Had it been Harrison I would have told him to pull himself together and cool off.'

'You saw them together quite often?'

'Yes.'

'How did he treat her?'

'In a sulky sort of way. And he was always jealous as far as I was concerned.'

'That's understandable. And how did she treat him when you were there?'

'When he was in a mood?—jokingly. She is a lively spirited woman.'

By then I had got a picture from the man,

and also a suspicion that Mr Franklyn was not an altogether honourable man.

'It seems the best thing for you to do is tell the police, or if you think your suspicion too vague, then wait and see if Harrison turns up at the office in the morning.'

'I hope you have been able to understand my agitation.'

'I can understand your agitation, but not why you came to me.'

'I felt I had to come to somebody and I knew she had been to you today.'

'Did she telephone you as soon as she had been here?'

'I think she did. She said you could not help her.'

'Would you be surprised to know that Mr Harrison also rang me for help?'

'Jim did?' He looked astonished.

'You are surprised!'

'A bit more than that. There is a strange weakness about Jim Harrison that I don't know enough about to let me explain to you.'

'What do you mean?'

'If ever I suggested he should get outside help to solve a personal problem of his, he wouldn't do it. It seemed to me he has some extraordinary guilt complex. He is always frightened that outsiders might find out the truth about him.'

'What truth?'

'God knows. He's been with us for nearly

twenty years, and that curious little guilt has shown now and again, but I've not had the slightest idea what it's about.'

'Well, thanks, Mr Franklyn. And what did you expect me to do about all this?'

'Find Geraldine. Make sure she's safe.'

'For Harrison's sake, Mr Franklyn?'

I watched him as he hesitated.

'No,' he said at last. 'For *hers*.'

2

He went after showing some dissatisfaction over my attitude, but did not try to overcome it.

I stood in the hall for a minute after he had gone, wondering what on earth I was being tied up in.

I had then been approached from three sides with different versions of what should have been the same story, none of which so far agreed with the first one I had overheard.

What was the truth about this proposed murder?

Where had the blood in the hall come from? Had there been an attack of some sort? On whom?

And what the hell was the motor-bike doing in the garage—smashed as she had first described—if it was supposed to be lying under her car just round the corner?

I went back into the kitchen. She wasn't there.

The back door is a garden door and nothing else. There had once been a tradesman's entrance through the end wall but later development had closed it off. Therefore the garden was a walled plot with no way out but back through the house.

The door to the room had been wide open all the time Franklyn had been with me, and I had faced the opening, so she could not have got out there.

She had to be in the house still. I went back to the hall.

'Mrs Harrison? Mrs Harrison! Are you upstairs?'

There was no answer.

I went back into the main living-room by way of the second door near the kitchen end of the passage. A quick search of the room showed nobody there either.

The only place she could have been was upstairs, but I did not know why she didn't answer my shout.

I went up to the top. There is a large bedroom, a small one and the bathroom in between. All the doors were open there, not for any sinister reason but because when I go from room to room I don't bother to shut them if I am alone. Just as I was beginning to think she had got out somehow, I found her.

Her clothes were tossed on a chair in my room. She was in my bed, fast asleep. She must have been exhausted to have gone off like that, but then, feeling a threat of murder creeping on must be very hard to bear for hours on end—

But as she slept she looked quite peaceful. There was no trace of tension about her face. She looked to be in a deep, normal sleep.

For a moment a strange cold feeling came up through me.

Suppose she was not sleeping? Suppose someone had got in before Franklyn arrived?

I went close to the bed and bent over. I could see then that she was breathing quietly.

My body changed from frozen to weak. I straightened up with a feeling of relief. The last thing I wanted in my sphere of life was a dead woman in my bed.

Or any woman, I amended. Or not at that time, I qualified.

I searched the room, for the idea somebody might have got in was still getting at the back of my mind. When I was sure nobody else was there, I went out and closed the door.

When I began to go down the stairs I heard something drop. The sound of a hard object falling on the tiled floor of the bathroom was quite clear.

I looked aside through the landing banisters. I could see straight along the bathroom floor and the fallen object, the top off a disinfectant bottle, lay where nothing had been before.

One does not normally keep defensive

weapons in the pockets of a dressing-gown, and I paused on the stairs wondering what to do. Never a hero, my instinct was to bolt downstairs and phone the police, but my sense of duty told me that before I bolted for the safety of my own skin, I should have a thought for Mrs Harrison.

If the husband had got in, then it was her he had his sights on, and if I went downstairs his way would be clear.

For a moment I wondered how I could have forgotten to look behind the bathroom door, and then with a shock I remembered that I had looked there. I had also looked behind the door of the spare bedroom, yet somebody was up in the bathroom.

I was then looking directly at a wall mirror on the tiled wall, and that, when I moved my head to one side, reflected behind the door and showed nobody there.

A number of explanations came into my head. Perhaps a change in temperature had caused the loose cap to pop itself off the disinfectant bottle. Such things do happen and give rise to thoughts of poltergeists.

But I had never had a poltergeist and I didn't fully believe my story about the change in temperature. I was really sure in my quaking heart that somebody was in the bathroom and keeping well down below the level of the mirror.

At that moment, a cat walked out. It was

not even a lucky black cat. It was a completely white cat, and it looked at me between the banisters as if I might be a mouse hardly worth considering.

I was so glad to see that cat. With it my fears of a secret man in the house fled. Until my memory recovered itself and I dimly remembered asking my daily woman to have the fanlight repaired.

The memory turned me cold again, and I went downstairs and to the fanlight above the back door. It had not been mended, but it had been stuck shut by the woman with a wedge of folded paper in the crack.

I looked at the cat, not quite so sure then that I was glad to see it. It brought back the question; how did it get in? I was quite sure it hadn't come in while I'd admitted my unwanted guests of the night. Perhaps it had been there all day. I went back into the kitchen and made more tea.

By then I was heartily sick of the Harrisons and all their friends, and yet I couldn't help questioning myself about them.

What were they up to? Could there really be a situation of a wife running from her murderous husband who went about warning people of what he was going to do? And would their friends be queuing up to tell me how close to the truth the threat of a murder could be?

And then, in the cloud of terror in which

she found herself, having been horrified, pursued and nerve-racked, she had gone upstairs, undressed, got into my bed and fallen into a peaceful sleep.

Impossible. One may fall down and sleep from sheer exhaustion after such torment, but one would be rather less than distraught to do what she had done and be sleeping so peacefully.

I think it was her calm appearance as she had slept which caused me surprise, then puzzlement, then doubt.

Added to that was the bike's being in the garage when she said it had pursued her. Yes, there were other bikes, but how many did the husband have instantly available? A car one might pick up anywhere, but bikes are not so common.

Then there was the matter which had arisen with Franklyn about the fake jewel. Apparently he accepted Harrison's story that it had been an error of judgement. Maybe. But suppose it wasn't? Had it replaced the genuine article? Harrison had had it in his house and might have arranged to have it copied there—

But that was drifting into byways of thought. My main consideration should have been to sort out just how it had come to pass that, in less than twenty-four hours, this matter had been overheard (by accident?), and then a series of people had begun calling on me to tell me the truth of a threatened murder, but each truth was different from the one before.

Each new detail in each story seemed to be the same, but had a different significance.

The only thing nobody had agreed on was the woman's status as a call-girl. That seemed to me to be important, because that was the stated reason for the husband's threat. Humiliation over years had been the keynote, combined with the usual jealousy.

Yet the man appeared to be a top-class buyer of antique jewellery, a trade world in which few humiliated men could survive, since it had to require sharpness and knowledge of both jewellery and below average human nature.

What on earth was the truth of it? Was the man trying to murder the peacefully sleeping lady upstairs? If so he was going about it all in a strange way indeed.

In fact, so was she.

Then we had Mr Franklyn, the responsible chief of the firm which traded in highly valuable things. He should have known his duty, if he feared anything, was to go to the police.

But he, like Mr Harrison, and Harrison's wife, feared the police because of some guilty secret.

What guilty secret? And whose was it? Who was protecting whom by not going to the police?

I poured another cup of tea and as I began to drink, posed myself a question which had been uneasily in the back of my mind for some hours.

Could this whole thing be some elaborate plot to involve me? But if so, what for?

At that stage in my ponderings I heard the cat miaow. I got up and went into the hall. The animal was moving slinkily from side to side of the front door, rubbing its neck against my umbrella stand at the end of each trip.

When I came into view she stopped, looked at me and mewed.

She wanted to go out, and she knew that was the way to go out, presumably because that was the way she had come in.

I went along to the front door. She watched with a little impatience as I turned the handle of the lock and pulled the door open.

From the bottom of my eye I saw her white body streak out past one corner of the doorway. She kept to the corner because in the middle stood a man, he had been so close to the panels I almost pushed him backwards as I was about to step out and sample the first grey, still air of daylight.

I looked at him. He looked aghast, like the ghost of Banquo turning up at the wrong dinner.

'Are you Mr Harrison?' I said.

'Yes. I was just going to knock.'
'Come in, for the Lord's sake.'
He did. I closed the door and thought, 'Well, I'm all right now, with the would-be murderer downstairs and his victim asleep upstairs!'

I wondered why I had asked him in and realised it was not because I wanted to prevent a murder, but because my curiosity had been stretched far enough.

CHAPTER FIVE

1

'How did you know my name?' he said.

'Didn't you ring me earlier? I recognised your voice.'

'Oh.' He seemed puzzled for a moment, even suspicious. 'I think I must have seen you before,' he added.

'One sees a lot of people. Mr Harrison, it's dawn. What do you want at such a time?'

'You will tell me at once to go to the police, Mr Keyes. I can't do that. If that means you think I am a dishonest man or a crook, so be it.'

'I hope you're not thinking of using me as a priest,' I said. 'I'm not qualified to hear confessions.'

'This is no confession. I've done nothing,

but there's more than a chance that the police would think I have. The way things look would give them a strong case against me.'

'Against you for what?'

'Murdering my wife.'

I had turned away impatiently, but then I turned back.

'You have murdered your wife?'

'No. But it will look like that.'

'Your wife is dead?'

'Yes.'

'Have you seen her body?'

'No.'

'Then how do you know she's dead?'

'She is missing. There is blood on the floor and a heavy rug has gone.'

I sat on the arm of a chair. I felt confusion getting into my head due, this time, to two stories beginning to coincide.

'Where do you live?'

'Hampton Court.'

'Tell me how it came about that you thought your wife had been murdered.'

He turned and began to walk towards the door. He turned again and came back.

'I've been at the end of my tether, Mr Keyes. Yesterday I told a very dear friend that I could see no way out but to do away with my wife.'

He looked at me as if expecting shock.

'Why was murder the only way out?'

My reaction startled him. For a moment he

did not seem to know what to do, but recovered and went on fast.

'She had provoked me beyond endurance. I became in such a state that murder did seem the only solution—' His voice faded, as if he were horrified by his own words.

'Well?'

'But after I'd got it off my chest I began to see that perhaps I had been foolish.'

'Foolish in telling your friend?'

'No. Foolish in thinking what I did.'

'You went back to your house at some time tonight?'

'At about midnight.'

'What did you intend to do then? Make it up with your wife?'

'No. I intended to try and make her see my point of view. I thought if I could do that it would remove the danger—'

'The danger that you might try and kill her?'

'Yes.'

'Tell me how you went into the house.'

'I used my key as usual. When I opened the door I was in a bad state of nerves. It needed some strength on my part to do what I had decided to do—try to show her why I had reached such a stage as to think of murder.'

'You would not have said that to her?'

'No. Of course not. I would have said violence, and that might have been enough. I am not a violent man. She would have known that.'

'You went in. And then?'

'I went in and half closed the door behind me. For some reason I left it a little ajar, as if planning an escape route in case the desire to murder got the better of my common sense. I was that badly frightened of my self-control.'

'What did you do? Call out?'

'Yes, but there was no answer, and I think it was then that I realised there was something odd about the place. I didn't see what it was at first, but as I looked along the hall I saw the garden door was wide open.

'I went along to it, and would have called out, but it seemed absurd to imagine Margaret would be out in the garden, in the darkness—'

'Margaret? Is that your wife's name?'

'Yes. Then I thought she might have gone out in her car. I went down the garden, and found the car gone, and a motor-bike of mine had been smashed against the wall, obviously by the car. The wide-open garden door and the clumsy getting out of the car indicated to me some sort of panic.

'I went back into the hall. Now there are steps up from the garden to the garden door, and as my eyes drew level with the hall floor I saw a pool of something shining brighter than the floor boards. It's an old oak floor and almost black.

'When I got inside and took a look, I could

see what it was. I also realised why the hall had looked odd. A big rug was missing. It had usually lain close to where the blood was.'

He stopped then as if too distressed to go on.

'What did you think had happened?'

'I thought she had been killed and her body taken away in the rug.'

'Why? Is that what you would have done?'

'No. In fact, when I was standing in the hall, almost petrified with shock, I realised that I could never have killed anyone.'

'But who might have done such a thing?' I said.

'She had a number of men friends,' he said. 'She used to play them one against the other. I had jealousy in my mind. I thought she had been murdered in the heat of the moment, then her body wrapped in the rug and taken out to the garage and driven away in the car.'

'That would leave a great many clues leading to a murderer, Mr Harrison.'

'I was merely guessing at what might have happened.'

'What did you do next?'

'I went upstairs to make sure she was not somewhere there. When I came downstairs again I looked in the kitchen and saw that she had been there.

'Then when I went back into the hall I saw one more thing missing—'

'The fireman's axe,' I said, and watched him.

He appeared to be shaken to his roots.

'How did you know? How did you know there was a fireman's axe?'

'I was told about it by Mr Franklyn.'

This time he was startled in quite another way.

'Franklyn? Do you know him?'

'He called here just before you. You must have seen him go.'

It was a wild shot and, like most such shots, it didn't come off.

'No, I didn't,' he said. 'Why did he come?'

'He came because he feared you might try and kill your wife.'

'What!'

'It seems your wife rang him yesterday afternoon, and said she was worried about the way you were behaving.'

He was shocked then.

'She did? Was it that noticeable?'

Of course it hadn't been that noticeable, probably, but to tell him the truth would have brought Mac the printer in as well.

'I suppose so,' I said. 'Tell me, in what way was your wife provocative? Have the men friends anything to do with that?'

'Very much so.'

'Do you know any of them?'

'Not that I know of.'

The day and the night had almost gone by

then, and what had started as a simple but distressing eavesdrop was becoming a conspiracy of several people all scared to death of the murder of a woman, and, of all the visitors, I alone knew she was safe, well, and fast asleep upstairs.

What was intriguing me by then was the way the stories seemed so similar, and yet none was the right one.

From that time it seemed to me that Harrison had boiled over in that confessional pew, when he had told Mac. But in telling, he had relieved the pressure on himself and given it to Mac, who had phoned Mrs Harrison expressing his fears, and she had come to me.

She had come to me because Mac had known who I was from the know-all barman, and so I had been visited by all the participants in this story, which hadn't happened, excepting Mac. But I had got to a stage then when I half expected him to turn up for breakfast.

The chain of events seemed to be: Harrison had told Mac, Mac had warned Mrs Harrison, she had come to me and then told Franklyn of her visit.

Why had she done that? I wondered. Were Franklyn and Mac both very close friends of hers? Or something more? Whichever they were, Harrison did not seem to put them down as her men friends as he had said he didn't know any of them.

'You do see my position, Mr Keyes? After what I've said, and the way I've acted—foolishly, but still—I should be suspected at once of my wife's murder.'

'Why are you so certain your wife is dead?'

'I'm not certain. But what would you make of the signs in the house?'

'Did you once play a joke on Mr Franklyn with some blood from the butcher?'

'A joke? No! I got it for the roses.'

'The roses?'

'I was told that it was first-class manure for rose-growers. I spilt some of it—I forget where now. Somebody saw it and had a nightmare on the spot. It was an utterly stupid incident. You're not suggesting it is pig's blood in the hall?'

'How do you know what it is, Mr Harrison?'

'I don't of course—'

A thunderbolt shattered our conversation holding both of us dead still in the room.

Through the open door we both heard Mrs Harrison's deep, soft and attractive voice.

'Mr Keyes! Are you down there?'

Harrison's eyes grew wide, then bulged like boiled eggs.

'My wife!' he said in strangled tones.

He turned suddenly and rushed out into the hall.

'Whore!' he shouted.

She said something which I didn't hear and he didn't want to. He came tearing back into the room, struggling to pull something out of his pocket.

I was on the point of trying to tell him he was quite mistaken in his view of what was afoot in my house, but felt it would not be appropriate.

It appeared less appropriate still when he produced an automatic pistol from his pocket and pointed it at me.

'I've had enough! Double-crossed! I'll stand no more of this!'

Of all the things which have happened to me in a curious life, having a gun pointed at me in my own house was the most petrifying. All my nerves froze up so that his frenzied actions seemed to take place in slow motion. I even seemed to see his finger tighten slowly on the trigger of that gun.

I had no idea what to do. I don't believe I even thought what I was doing when I picked a heavy cushion off the sofa and swung it across so that it hit his arm with the gun in it.

I heard the gun fire but I was so frightened I feel now that if I had been hit I wouldn't have felt it.

The cushion fell to the floor and the gun, inexplicably, on top of it.

Harrison stood there staring at me and then put his hands to his face and burst into tears.

I sat down on the sofa because my legs were

too weak to keep on standing up.

2

Mrs Harrison came in wearing my dressing-gown. Practical as women usually are, she picked up the gun before her husband could get at it again.

'Have you all gone mad?' she said, her voice shaking with fright or anger or both. 'What on earth are you doing? Where did you get this damn gun, Jim? Jim! Pull yourself together!'

The man got a grip on his sobbing and turned his back on us.

'What the hell have I done now? I didn't want to shoot anybody! What the hell—!'

'Where did you get it?' she said again.

'A man approached me about a shady deal to do with jewellery. He got it for me.'

She waited a moment before she spoke again.

'Did you do this shady deal?'

'No.' He turned back to face us. 'It went against my instincts, though he offered a lot of money.'

'Did you get this to kill me?' She spoke very calmly, as if asking if he would like cereal for breakfast.

He shook his head.

'For God's sake, Maggie! Would I do that? No—I bought it because I felt too much was getting known about me keeping so much stuff in the house. I thought once he knew I had it he'd spread the word round and put people off trying to burgle us.'

'Why did you bring it here?'

'I got it at home when I went into the house tonight. I feared someone was in there. I thought you were dead.' The last sentence was uttered almost in a whisper.

She looked puzzled then and glanced aside at me.

'You knew I wasn't dead! You followed me here!'

'I thought you were dead!' he repeated. He sounded angry.

She stared.

'Who would have killed me if you wouldn't?'

He sat down in a chair very suddenly.

'I'm going crazy,' he said.

'How did you get here from your house?' I said.

He looked up, as if for a moment he didn't understand.

'In my car—rather the firm's car. How else would I have got here?'

'The motor-bike—' she said.

'It's smashed,' he said. 'You must have hit it.'

'A motor-bike followed me here,' she said, blankly. 'A bike was behind me all the way. In the end, I hit it. He came by to stop me. I thought—I was in danger. I hit the bike and got out and ran. The man started to follow—I got here first.'

He was staring at her in alarm.

'What man? What do you mean—followed you? All this way? Ten miles or more—?'

They looked at each other then. I wondered just how deep was the rift between them, because it didn't show much in the way they looked at each other.

I think that for the first time the idea came to me that here was a pair of irresponsible loonies who didn't understand themselves, and certainly not each other.

'Perhaps he wasn't chasing you at all,' I said. 'But if he wasn't he certainly would have started once you smashed his bike. But that is not my affair. What is my affair is that I have been shot at by a man with a loaded gun in my own house. What do you propose I should do about that?'

'I was in a state of hysteria,' he said. 'What's the good of pretending? I just lost my head.'

'And I nearly lost mine,' I pointed out.

'I think you had better take this,' Mrs Harrison said, and gave me the gun.

I handled it carefully. I don't like guns, and I made sure the safety-catch was firmly in the off position, before I got up and locked it in a drawer of a small writing-table.

'You're not going to tell the police?' she said.

'I ought to tell a psychiatrist,' I said. 'I've been kept up all night and half yesterday for something that never happened and, from what I can see, never will happen. You are a couple of the dedicated insane and I'm a certifiable idiot for ever having listened—'

It was at that moment that I wondered where the bullet had gone. I stood up and looked round. I had been standing by the big chair from which I had snatched the cushion, so the bullet should have gone into the left-hand corner of the room.

The idea of looking for the bullet came into my head at the same time as that of talking to the police about the gun, because one thing I do not favour is loose guns in this world.

The idea of looking for the bullet, therefore, was protective.

I searched the corner of the room but found no damage at all.

I went back to where I had got the cushion in case the shot had gone into the soft furniture when the gun had been swept aside.

There was no hole.

'The bullet wasn't there,' I said. 'It was a blank cartridge. Did you know that?'

Instead of taking that way out and making an apologetic joke and saying, 'I'm sorry, but I only meant to scare you,' or something of that nature, the idiot said, 'Blank? No!'

'So you really meant to shoot me!' I said.

'I was off my head. I was jealous. I just

didn't think—'

She got up then and came to me.

'Please don't go to the police! *Please!*'

Thus she pleaded for the husband she had said, for eight hours or so, had planned to kill her.

Could anybody really be that barmy? Could anyone really turn round that fast?

He was sitting there staring at nothing.

'Somebody was killed there tonight,' he said dully, and then looked up. 'Perhaps that's why you were followed! He thought you'd seen it!' He stood up.

'Look here!' I protested. 'If you've had a murder in your house you've got to overcome your fastidious objections and go to the police! If you don't, you may be next on the list for the very reason you've just given. The murderer will be scared you saw something.'

Harrison began to march about.

'How the hell has all this happened to us? Who's behind it? Somebody must be! Somebody must be doing something to bust us. But what for? What the hell have we done? What the hell have *we* done?'

He had clearly forgotten where he was. The man was right in saying he was at the end of his tether, but it seemed to me it had been stretched for a very long time.

And looking at the two together, I began to disbelieve the story I had overheard him telling Mac the printer. There was something missing from that wretched story that was here plainly for me to see.

That thing was affection.

Yet only hours before, I had heard the awful story of a man goaded into the brink of murder. More recently still I had heard the wife telling me she feared that very act.

How much of those stories held together? The call-girl epic fitted with the refusal of hotels to admit her when she was on her own. He had also told of men friends. Franklyn was clearly a close friend, and Mac, too. Both had leapt in to protect her as far as they could without themselves being suspected by Harrison.

But this case was surely something more than jealousy and exasperation over a wanton intransigence in the lady? It was certainly something more than a sudden fear of a husband running amok.

But what? Not for the first time that shadow stole into my mind, like the phantom at the feast; a sudden consideration for my own part in the affair.

Mac knew who I was. Was it remotely possible that the heart-rending story in the pub pew had been specially concocted and acted for my benefit? It had been followed by the wife's visit, then her frantic reappearance late at night, then Franklyn, then, at last, the husband.

Whichever way I looked at that, the whole

circus was centred on me. But could that have been deliberate? And if so what on earth for? Why me?

What reason could there be for a man's deliberately broadcasting a story about his wife's commercial infidelity and his intention to murder her?

Of course, I had the two main movers in the plot right there in the room, but they were the last people on earth who would be willing to enlighten me.

I became impatient with my own inability to do anything in my favour.

'What are you two proposing to do now?' I said. 'Tell me.'

'What do you mean, Mr Keyes?' the woman said quietly.

'Well, are you proposing to go home, kiss and make up or wave goodbye with the fireman's axe?'

She looked at me.

'Is there anyone waiting outside?' she said.

I went to the windows and pulled the cords. Daylight came in through the lacery of the curtains after the big folds were pulled back. I looked out. There was a milk float at the end of the mews and a man leaning against the garden wall which flanked the mews on the far side. He was reading a paper.

'Come and look,' I said.

She came to my side.

'Do you know him?' I said, pointing to the

newspaper reader. 'He's wearing leathers. He might be your motor-cyclist.'

She stared.

'I can't see his face,' she said.

'Harrison!' I said, for I was angry by then, 'come and look!'

He came and looked. For a moment he just stood there and then the man outside lowered the paper to turn to another page and his face was clear to see.

'Hell, yes!' he said. 'I know him!'

The woman turned her head and looked at her husband with a frown.

'Who is it?' she said.

He did not bother to answer her.

'Is there a back way out of this house?' he said.

'No,' I said.

He swore briefly but with considerable force.

CHAPTER SIX

1

I didn't bother to ask Harrison any questions about the man outside. I was tired and overstrained with the night's peculiar events.

'Go into the kitchen and stay there,' I told them. 'Make some tea and toast. Anything you fancy. I'm going to get up.'

I went upstairs, leaving them to get on with some kind of breakfast. I was tired of asking questions to which I never got an answer which did not confuse the issue more.

A shower and shave improved my physical wellbeing, which eased my mind from constant tautness over the extremely confusing case of the Harrisons.

If they had been confusing it by themselves, it might have been easier to see through, but why Franklyn? And who was the man outside in motor-cycling gear?

A genuine cyclist, having had his bike smashed up, would not be hanging about outside pretending to be picking out winners from the racing pages. A genuinely aggrieved person, knowing whither the guilty party had fled, would have come banging on my door.

Yet he stood outside, waiting.

When I went downstairs dressed and refreshed, I felt clearer in the head and decided to take the points to which I wanted the answer in the order I proposed and no other.

She had made tea, coffee and toast. I had tea and toast.

'Earl Grey is all right for the middle of the night, but Assam is best in the morning,' I said.

'Of course,' she said, regretfully.

He looked as if he did not understand, or could not bring his mind to bear on a matter of such unimportance.

'I want the address and the keys to your house,' I said.

'You are going there?' she said, with a trace of uneasiness.

'I mean to get one thing cleared up today.' I held my hand out for the key.

Harrison handed over a key fob. He pointed out the necessary key. His finger was shaking.

'This man outside scares you?' I said. 'Why?'

'Because I don't know who he is,' Harrison said.

'But your wife smashed up his bike. She said so.'

'No. It isn't that,' she said.

Then the idea came to me that if I left them to stew in extreme anxiety for a while, they might be the readier to talk sensibly when I got back.

'You'd better stay in the back of the house. Don't go into the front rooms at all. The cleaner doesn't come till this afternoon. You'll be on your own till then, but I'll be back long before.'

'What if somebody calls?' she said.

'Don't answer the door!' I said, exasperation beginning to rise again.

I drank tea and ate some buttered toast. When I had done I went into the hall and the living-room. Through the curtains I could see the newspaper reader still in position though as I watched, I saw him lower his paper slightly and stare towards the house. He angled his left wrist so he could see his watch, then once more looked towards the house before going on with his reading.

He made me uneasy. I looked round towards my writing-desk, then out at the reader once more. There was a quiet menace about a man persistently waiting and watching outside the house and, for all I knew, he might have been there for hours before dawn.

Harrison had even suspected somebody might be outside, waiting for him in an unpleasant sort of way.

I went to the desk, unlocked the drawer and took out the automatic pistol. My experience of guns was not great, but I had learnt that it does not greatly matter if a gun is filled with blanks or has no bullets at all; the fact that you point it at someone usually gets results.

I put the gun into my pocket and went back to the kitchen.

'Are you going to feel safe while I'm gone?' I asked.

'That man can't get in here, can he?' Harrison said, sharply.

'I wasn't bothered about the man,' I said. 'You seem to have forgotten this lumpish story you tried to get me to swallow last night.'

The woman looked up quickly then. The man frowned.

'What story?' he said, in a dry voice.

'I'm sorry you've forgotten,' I said with quiet irony, I hoped. 'But if I come back and your wife is dead, I shall understand how it came about, Mr Harrison.'

They didn't say a word as I went out. I slammed the front door and unlocked the garage next to it. From the corner of my eye I could see the man still standing by the wall a short way down the mews. He seemed to be watching me as I unlocked the doors.

I got into the car, started up and backed out, swinging round so that the car backed past the man by the wall. I stopped with my window opposite him.

'Are you from the Gas Board?' I said.

He frowned.

'No.'

'I thought you might be waiting for your mate,' I said. 'There's serious trouble in my house. I rang the office, but it seems I'd better go round there before the house blows up.'

I drove off. As I slowed down to join the road running past the end of the mews, I looked in the mirror and saw him stuffing his paper into his pocket as he walked away from where he had been.

The explosive story seemed to have caught

his interest.

His rapid departure from the scene—either from fear of explosion or because he thought I had recognised him—made me quite sure he was an underling. It was likely he had left his post for one of the reasons I have said, but, also, to find out what he ought to do next.

The idea that there might be some kind of gang or small organisation behind the mystery of the Harrisons had come into the back of my mind before. As I drove out west I kept such a notion well back. I couldn't see what the incipient murder story had to do with organised crime.

The house was quite beautiful. It was a Regency bijou riverside residence at the end of a terrace of similarly beautiful small houses, facing an open stretch of common and backing almost on to the river.

I parked a way off and walked through a passage made by a break between two terraces of houses to a path, flanked on the waterside by a green stretch of open space. It was very easy to see which was the Harrisons' garage of the small number there opening on to the road.

The Harrisons' doors were still open, showing only a somewhat bent motor-bike inside. I went in, closed the doors after me, from there I knew my way from the several descriptions I had been given by my various visitors.

The back door of the house was shut when I got there, and as it was self-locking, I used the key.

When I walked slowly into the hall the house did not give the instant feel of an empty one. It was almost as if Mrs Harrison was still somewhere there.

I looked along towards the floor by the stairs where, I had been twice told, there was blood and a missing rug.

When I looked there was no blood and there was a large Persian rug.

It might not be the same rug as the one usually there, I realised, and blood might have been cleaned up, of course—

By whom?

Harrison, surely, had been the last person to leave the house that night. He had not said anything about clearing up. According to his story he would have been in no state to wait behind and clear up.

I looked at the wall by the door.

There was a leather skeleton holster for a fireman-type axe, but no axe. That, at least, agreed with what they had said.

During the next few minutes I looked into every room in the house. It was one of the most beautifully furnished I had ever seen, all in matching Regency and Napoleonic style.

I paused on the landing and thought about it. My original view, taken from overhearing the distressed husband, of a suburban villa drama had gone altogether. The house alone was worth a great deal of money and the contents worth more still. In all it could be regarded by some as representing a small fortune.

On top of that the husband was a dealer, in jewellery, not known generally as an impoverishing trade for those in it. Those entrusted to buy valuables, probably in cash, wouldn't be on a starvation wage.

I sat on a chair by a Regency table on the landing and gazed out of the landing window at the common and the trees of the great park beyond.

It was difficult to apply almost any of the original overheard story to this layout. The idea of the husband unable to buy his wife a coat, when they lived in a place like this, did not fit at all. She could have sold two chairs and got enough for a mink or anything else she wanted.

If she had traded as a call-girl, then it could only have been because she liked it. To pretend that any couple with property like this would need to trade themselves for cash was idiotic.

There was one oddity I had noticed in my tour and that was I had not seen any letters anywhere. No bills, accounts or anything addressed to the Harrisons. There was a phone book in the bedroom. I looked up the book for the Harrisons but the house was not listed.

The Harrisons could be ex-directory, or using a business name instead of their own.

It was at that moment I fancied I heard someone moving downstairs.

A fantasy thought came into my head that perhaps I had the wrong house, or that I had the right house but that there were no Harrisons.

I went out on to the landing and looked down into the hall. It looked as empty as before. I listened and heard nothing down there.

Perhaps the sound had been water in the pipes, or some settlement in the old building making a creak, as perhaps it had creaked for two hundred years.

When I turned to go down the stairs again I heard another sound of movement below.

Remembering the white cat, I wondered if there was such an animal in the house, but I had noticed no saucers or water-bowl in the kitchen for such a pet.

I stood quite still and listened. For a reason I could not determine, I began to feel almost certain that someone was downstairs in the house and trying not to let me know it.

I remembered the somewhat frightening account of Mrs Harrison's time in the house last night. I felt again the tension she had created in me when telling her story. Almost as if I had been there.

And now I was there, and there was somebody downstairs not wanting to be heard. As I listened to the intense silence I became more sure that the quiet was artificial. Whoever was in the house had, perhaps, stopped breathing to be sure I could not hear them.

It was then that I remembered the gun I had brought, a stage piece with its blank shots, but enough to dissuade most people from intended evil.

I kept my hand on it in my pocket as I went slowly, and very quietly, down the stairs and into the hall.

2

The place looked empty. It sounded empty. I thought I could hear my heart beating loudly in the quiet.

The doors were open all around. I looked in one room after the other and each was empty. I began to think I must be wrong; that the woman's story was too much in my mind.

And yet, how could I be sure? A man might move from one room to another behind me. I did not know for sure what doors might open between rooms. And there was a cellar somewhere underneath me as I stood, listening, by the stairs.

Perhaps the sounds had come from below. There was a door under the staircase which I had seen when coming in at the back door. I went along to it very quietly and listened again.

I heard nothing, but more than ever I felt sure that someone was hiding quite near me at that moment.

The cellar door was shut. I began to doubt whether I could have heard anything through it and looked around me once more.

Just ahead and to my left was the kitchen door. It had been open but as I watched, it began to close very, very slowly. For a moment I was not quite sure it was moving, the action was so gradual. There was no sound.

For several seconds I just stood still, watching the snail-like movement of the door, and then I took the gun out of my pocket. I looked at it, then put back the safety catch, just in case I needed to fire off a couple of warning shots.

I was torn between two urgent curiosities; one concerning the kitchen door and what moved it, and the other, testing a feeling of almost certainty that someone was behind the cellar door.

Anything could make a door move slowly; a draught, a settlement of the house, a spider's little engineering altering the status quo.

I got hold of the handle of the cellar door, turned it and pulled the door open.

A man stood behind it, his attitude one of

menace, because he also had a gun in his hand.

'Hold it right there, brother!' he said and pointed the gun.

Instinctively, I pulled my trigger and the gun kicked back in my grip. There was a hell of a crack. The man looked surprised, and stood quite still, it seemed, for several seconds. Then he began to bend in the middle. I thought he was coming towards me and stepped back.

I realised that in firing a blank I had also shot my bolt. The gun was useless once he knew it wasn't really loaded.

But instead of attacking me, he dropped his gun, then began to topple forwards, tried to recover and then stepped shakily back. He slipped on the top step of the cellar stairs and then went tumbling down, crashing and bumping as if he was breaking up the wood in the descent.

At what point my startled mind grasped the fact that the shot had not been a blank, I'm not sure. Looking back it seemed to have been almost a minute I stood there, listening for the man to move.

There was only silence from the black depths of the cellar.

I saw a switch on the wall inside the door and snapped it on. Light flooded the stairs and a cellar, scattered with crates and boxes, apparently just thrown down there when finished with.

The man lay sprawled amongst the boxes half face down over one crate and his legs, curiously distorted in attitude, on the floor.

I could see blood spreading over the yellow wood of the crate under him. I also saw his gun lying on the stairs, two steps down.

No expert in gunnery, I yet recognised the short-nosed Smith and Wesson .38; a type I had seen before in the course of my work, but never handled.

I went down a few stairs. It was very still down there.

There really was no need to make any close examination, because one seems to know when death happens and it had happened to that burly fellow just a little sooner than he had intended it should happen to me.

Murder and the examination of dead bodies does not normally come into my range of work; that sort of thing goes to the police.

But the circumstances here were very different from the usual, beginning with the fact that, technically, I had murdered him, and I needed time and a few facts to help me think out what in hell I was going to do about it.

I made sure he was dead. I looked in his outside pockets and found only a used envelope with some ballpoint jottings on the back of it. The address on the front was:

'Mr D. Kelly,
1017, Lakeward Ave.,
Cleveland, Ohio.'

That might have been the dead man's name and address, or it might have been somebody else's. The interesting thing about it was that it was an internal US letter, postmarked Baltimore, Maryland, a week before.

The furniture upstairs connected with the American in my mind and I thought he might have been a dealer who had come to see Harrison on some deal—or to blow his head off and not bother about dealing.

The inner breast pocket was not accessible to me, not so much because he lay partly on it, but because it was soaked in blood. I looked around the cellar. There were quite a number of crates and boxes, some still with pieces of furniture in them, but mostly opened and left empty.

Then I found a surprising thing. There was a door in the cellar wall and it was not a cupboard door, but a heavy outside type of door, with locks and bolts.

I pushed my way between some crates and reached it. The bolts were drawn back and the big key in the lock was in the unlocked position.

It looked as if this might be the American's point of entry. In which case Mrs Harrison was right and there could have been someone else in the house the previous night, without her knowing how anyone could have got in.

But the story was they had lived in the house some years and therefore they must have known of such a door in the cellar.

Also, the bolts had been drawn and the key turned from the inside of the building.

I opened the door. There was a set of brick steps going up apparently to the garden, but the entrance was overgrown with ivy and other weeds and the daylight broke through only when light breeze rustled the leaves.

It was a direct entry into the cellar from the back garden, the way coal had once been delivered, but it did not look as if it was much used at that time. Most of the weeds were fresh, enthusiastic young growths.

I closed the door and returned to my immediate problem which I instinctively wanted to duck.

There was a dead man lying around and I had killed him. True, I hadn't expected anything of the sort, but carrying a gun as I had, I should have looked and made sure what sort of rounds were in the magazine. As it was I had played a blind game of Russian roulette and blown a man into the far lands as a result.

But then, he had also had a gun and it had pointed at me, and so there was a good case for self-defence.

Further, I was in the house legally.

And there I stopped. For was I legally

there? True, the house tied in with the Harrison stories and he had had a key, but the absence of any letters or bills or name in the phone directory all worried me. Of course, the Harrisons might have no bills, or everything paid by the bank, and name kept out of the directory. All these things were possible and not that unusual, but for the fact of Harrison's business. The sort of thing he engaged in surely would have needed that any interested buyer or seller would be able to get in touch with him directly?

But he might not deal that way.

It was a waste of nervous energy thinking around the matter like that. It was enough that I had been asked to take part in this insane case and given the keys of the house.

That was easily proved, for I had a whole wallet of keys and it would be straightforward to find which places those keys fitted, and so the link with the house established with Harrison and his business.

Right. The police would accept that. But why was I wandering around with a real gun even if I thought it only contained blanks? Which it didn't, but I had been wary of the man watching the house and feared attack.

Right. But how did the gun come to be in my house? Why, that was simple. The enraged and jealous husband came with a gun specifically to shoot me. How on earth could I say that? I would sound as crazy as the rest of them in this affair.

Because he had come to shoot me with a blank shot, and that was why I had taken the gun—

No. This was not going to stand up anywhere as a defence. I had deliberately taken a gun, not knowing what was in it.

I was in the Hampton house legitimately as far as I believed, and while there had been threatened by a man with a gun. By the sheer good fortune of having the gun with me—

I could almost see the learned judge beginning to fidget as this story went on.

There was also another small point, and that was I had never been appointed to deal with this case anyhow. Mrs Harrison had called privately, and then Franklyn, and then Harrison himself, and it had occurred to me before then that there might have been some underhand scheme to get me into something for their good and my detriment, though I had not been able to guess what such a scheme might be, or why it should have been conceived.

The first glimmerings of common sense began to return. I took note of the time so that I would be able to say exactly when this encounter had taken place.

My notebook is always in my pocket and I made a rough sketch of the cellar and its contents, and jotted some notes of possible excuses which I might use to masquerade as a defence.

Most of the time I am not essentially dishonest, but when shocked into a situation I never saw coming, I am inclined to use immediate invention in the hope of relief.

The man had been immediately behind the door when I had opened it, and he had been waiting there, I was sure.

To make absolutely certain I went carefully up the wooden stairs and no less than three of the twelve treads squeaked or groaned on the way up. I tested that twice with the same result, so it was then certain he must have been at the top, and waiting behind the door to surprise me.

He had also had a gun in his hand. I looked at that weapon as I passed it twice, but did not touch it.

When I reached the top the second time I turned and looked down at the dead man. Then I got out my notes and sat down on the top step to read them through.

It was then, as my forearm rested on my knee, that I saw a hole in my right sleeve of the jacket.

It was an oval sort of hole and looked dark round its edges. I jumped up and stood, almost stunned with surprise at the discovery.

'My God!' I cried aloud. 'I've been shot!'

And then I laughed with relief.

CHAPTER SEVEN

1

I gazed at the hole in my sleeve almost with affection, then got up from the stairs and looked at the wall by the garden door. It was not very difficult to see where the bullet had gone into the plaster, making a hole in the striped wallpaper.

The two holes were proof of self-defence. I felt a little easier, but very dry.

I was dry because I was partly shattered by the shocking surprise of the occurrence, and when I saw a half empty bottle of brandy on a kitchen shelf I poured some into a squat tumbler, put some water in it and drank with a feeling of gratitude.

The act of drinking calmed my nerves. I didn't know the gun was loaded. A classic phrase from comic songs and stories, but I just had not imagined anybody loading a gun with a mixture of blanks and shots. It seemed a macabre joke, but as it had happened it probably saved my life.

Mr Kelly had not been joking when he had shot at me. When I looked at the hole in my sleeve again I felt suddenly weak at the knees. That shot had been really very close.

I sat down at the table and did some quiet, deep breathing which a yoga follower had once assured me could soothe the nervous system quicker than anything.

But there were too many questions popping in my mind like fireworks in the sky. Who was Kelly? What had he been doing hiding in the cellar? Had the rug and bloodstain evidence been rectified? If so, by whom? If not so, why had the Harrisons and Franklyn lied? What on earth was the truth about the story of the pursuing motor-cycle? Was the man outside my house the rider? Then why hadn't he knocked and kicked up a fuss? If he was a crook and didn't dare, how did it come he was standing right outside for a long time for anybody to see him?

And what about the proposed murder? I had seen signs of affection remaining between the Harrisons which had made me sure that no murder had ever been seriously contemplated.

Then why the rigmarole in the pub pew? That outburst had had a deep effect on me, as it must have had on Franklyn and Mac the printer, for both had been anxious enough to fear murder.

And then a possible solution occurred to me.

Perhaps the woman at my house was *not* Mrs Harrison.

But if that were the case where was the real Mrs H? *Had* she been murdered already?

At about that point I realised that I was just

trying not to think about Kelly. In a while I would have to tell the police. The thought made my inside go cold.

I had a feeling that it would be more difficult than it seemed to me to persuade them of my innocence.

Suppose the rest of the bullets were real ones? Who was going to believe there had been just one blank in a magazine otherwise full of sound shots?

And as I came to that point, I wondered how any man could have walked about with a gun full of such lethal things and only one blank.

I used my handkerchief when I examined the gun again and clicked out the magazine. I did not want to leave fingerprints on the magazine and leave another difficulty to be got over in explanations to the police.

The bullets looked to me to be real, but I did not get them all out in my hand, and with a handkerchief, it might not be that easy to put them back. I replaced the magazine and got up.

I felt I should ring the police, but I was very uneasy over the fact I had brought the gun at all.

When I went out into the hall my will to find the phone quailed, and I thought I would take another look at the late Mr Kelly, just to make sure he hadn't come to life again.

Then with swiftly rising hope, I thought

perhaps I might have been wrong, and that he had been only wounded and knocked unconscious.

That I could have kept such a hope in my mind even for a second when I knew damned well the man was dead as mutton showed the strength of my will to try and wriggle out of a difficulty.

I even got to opening the cellar door and looking down again.

Then I stood quite still and felt cold all over.

There was no dead Kelly down there. He and the bloodstained crate had both gone.

For several seconds I must have stood frozen with this new shock, but I thought more calmly than I felt and realised the door from cellar to the garden must have been the way he had gone.

Then I realised he could not have gone alone and, as he was dead at the time, there must have been a second man somewhere who had removed the body.

But the crate as well?

The crate was bloodstained. Blood had soaked into it and so, perhaps, it had been taken with Kelly.

Somebody was trying to hide the fact that Kelly had been shot dead.

I went down the steps to the bottom and looked around on the floor. There was no blood around the brick floor that I could see, and the stained crate was nowhere in the cellar. I looked for it and made sure it had gone.

At the top of the stairs I sat down again and tried to sort out my thoughts. Into my mind came thoughts of the CIA, the KGB and whatever other underhand institutions might do this sort of thing.

Perhaps Kelly had been taken because he should not have been in the country. It was clear from the envelope that he must have arrived within the past day or two. Perhaps he had been an agent, or an international crook. There were a dozen things he might have been and none of them legal.

All ideas of calling the police had gone from me. I was anxious that with Kelly's death menace had not been removed. There was another man about that place.

The importance of that made me get up, back out into the hall, shut the cellar door and turn the mortice bolt.

As I did that I rememberd the rug and the bloodstain in the hall, both of which, according to legend, had been removed and then replaced without trace of bloody murder.

Now the crate had been taken, perhaps for the same reason; to pretend no murder had happened.

Had there been a murder in the hall that night? Had it been covered up after the evidence had been seen by Franklyn?

There are attempts to hide murders, but these are usually made by the murderer. In Kelly's case I was the killer, yet my murder had been covered up for me.

I went to the garden door and looked out through the upper glass panel. The garden was deserted, but beyond the low roof of the garages I saw the top of a furniture removal van.

It moved away as I watched, but it had been stopped by the Harrisons' garage when I first spotted it.

It was probably the late Mr Kelly's improvised hearse. I felt strangely grateful for it and went back to find the phone once more.

When I got the number the phone rang and rang for more than a minute, but I let it go on. The Harrisons were afraid to answer, but if it went on they might break down and pick up the instrument.

In the end I gave up and decided it would be best to go back and confront them with what had happened, because I had more than a suspicion by that time the Harrisons were right into whatever evil was going on in that place.

It might even have been that they had left the house that night so as to be right away from such evil and with an alibi.

And then came the recurring realisation that I, and not some outsider, had actually killed Kelly. True he had threatened me with his gun, but I had killed him.

But what had he been doing there? I felt the Harrisons would know and I badly wanted them to tell me what they did know.

As I turned away from the phone I caught a glimpse of a man watching the house. He was under a tree on the other side of the road, about five yards on to the common.

He had no newspaper. He was blatantly staring at the house.

As I watched he walked forward to the side of the road, looked up and down it, then crossed to the pavement outside the house.

He came into the garden and began to mount the steps up to the front door.

I was no longer anxious to stand around protesting my right to be in the house. I had had trouble enough already by then, so I turned, went through to the back door, opened it and went out. As I closed the door I heard the front door bell ringing.

Quietly and quickly I went down through the garden, into the garage and out of it on the other side, closing and locking both doors behind me.

I felt a lot easier as I made my way along to my car at the end of the alley. It had been a thoroughly unpleasant morning, thus far.

As I turned into the road by the side of the common and went to my car, the man who had rung the bell came towards me from the other direction.

He was looking directly at me as if he meant us to meet.

As he came nearer I felt there was something familiar about him, but could not recognise what the something was.

He stopped in front of me as I went to step off the pavement and go round to open the door.

'Excuse me,' he said.

He had a peculiarly searching look which made me uneasy. I thought he might be a police detective, but could not very well ask directly.

'Yes?' I said.

'I'm looking for Mrs Harrison,' he said abruptly.

'I'm sorry,' I said and smiled helplessly. 'I can't help you.'

'I believe that you know where she is,' he said firmly.

'I don't. Who are you?'

'I'm a friend of hers. She asked me to call this morning. I called twice. I believe the bell didn't ring the first time. I didn't hear it. I thought I heard a shot.'

He stared at me directly.

'A shot? What do you mean?'

'I heard a pistol shot. It came from somewhere in the house.'

'Good heavens! Why didn't you fetch the police? Which house was it?'

'You know perfectly well which house it is, Mr. Keyes. You were inside at the time.'

We looked at each other for several seconds. My memory was refreshed by the tone of his voice and I remembered where I had seen and heard him, though the seeing had been mostly covered by the back of Harrison's head.

'You are Mr Maclean, printer,' I said.

'Yes.'

'Let's get in the car,' I said.

2

I drove away from Hampton and stopped by the river. A pair of rowing skiffs were practising on the water.

'Why did you call at the house?' I asked watching the slim boats.

'I thought Mrs Harrison was there. I am a close friend.'

'What is Mrs Harrison's name?'

'Geraldine. Why are you asking this?'

'I need to know. You know who I am and I think you know what I do. I need to know because I have the feeling I have been tricked into a very difficult situation.'

'By the Harrisons?' he said quickly.

'Yes. And perhaps a third party.'

'Who?'

'I'm not sure yet. You are a close friend of Mr Harrison?'

'Of both of them.'

'Have you ever had a feeling that Harrison might want to murder his wife?'

Maclean laughed suddenly.

'I shouldn't think so.'

'You don't remember he ever said he might?'

'Harrison is a man of very sudden moods. He says things one moment and forgets them the next.'

'Mr Maclean, I heard him telling you that he would murder her.'

He was silent. The boats were like beetles in the distance.

'The man was rambling,' he said. 'I tried to put him off talking like that, but I don't believe he was serious. Would you believe it if an old friend suddenly said the same thing to you?'

'It depends on the circumstances. How much was he worried?'

'He was very worried, but about a business matter. When things went wrong for him he imagined everything round him was working for his destruction. He got into very bad troughs.'

'What does Mrs Harrison look like?'

'What does she look like? She's dark—well, her hair's a dark brown, and she's about five foot six or seven, very good figure, and pretty—at times quite beautiful.'

'You are fond of her?'

'In what way?'

'In any way.'

'I am fond of both of them. I have known them a long time.' He paused and then went on. 'One had to be very careful in showing fondness, Mr Keyes. Harrison is jealous, sometimes to the point of insanity. He even makes up wild stories about his wife's infidelity, as if he gets a kick out of feeding his own jealousy.'

'He's unbalanced?'

'In that degree, yes. But so many people are split. He is one. He is quite brilliant at his job, and there's no temper shown there. You might say he is a good poker player and can't be bluffed. Then he turns round on his wife and invents stories to try and prove she is bluffing him.'

'How do they get on, with this kind of jealousy breaking in?'

'She is used to it and lets it go by. He likes her to do that because it confirms his trumped-up suspicions and he gets more Russian in his gloomy fury.'

'But how do these storms end between them?'

He laughed shortly.

'I've never been present, Mr. Keyes. I can only imagine that it ends in wild reconciliation, which, for all I know, may be the purpose of his tormenting himself.'

'Like banging oneself on the head.'

'Nice when you leave off. I suppose so.'

'And you think that he does it because he enjoys the suffering?'

'I suppose that's it.'

'It isn't a put-up job for other people's entertainment?'

He looked at me then.

'I'd never thought of that,' he said. 'But now you mention it, he is inclined to the melodramatic on quite different matters. A lot of our friends believe it's his Russian mother.'

'She was a Russian?'

'She escaped and came over here sometime after the last war.'

'Is she still alive?'

'I couldn't say.'

I looked in the mirror. A car was parked some distance behind us. A curious thought came into my head that the occupants might be watching us.

It could have been the traumatic events in the Hampton house which gave me such jumpy notions, but after Kelly's vanishing act I knew perfectly well that something bigger than the Harrisons was in this affair, and I began to suspect it might be international, though I put aside the mental problem of trying to fit it in with the Harrison stories.

'Harrison goes abroad a good deal in his work?' I said.

'To Europe. Yes, he does. But not anywhere else, so far as I know. The heart of

that kind of business is in the European countries. Mr Keyes—' He stopped on the point of asking a question.
'What?'
'I want to see inside their house.'
'You've seen it before, as a close friend.'
'Indeed. But I'd like to see it because I believe something may have changed in there.'
I looked in the mirror again. This was an opportune moment to test my unspoken fear.
'Right,' I said. 'We'll go back.'
I drove off slowly to a turning on the right, fifty yards along the road. As we turned the corner I glanced aside. The car was starting off from the kerb, heading in our direction.
'What is Harrison's company car? Do you know?'
'Yes. A Rover. White.'
The car behind was a black BMW.
'Did you bring any friends with you?' I said.
'No.'
'Somebody's following us—or me. Where is your car?'
'Close to the house.'
'We'll go to the garage entrance. It's a quieter road. We might be able to see who it is.'
He turned and looked back.
'It's not very close behind,' he said.
I looked in the mirror. It was not close, but

it didn't have to be so long as it could see us.

'Have you got the keys to the house?'

'Yes.' I did not explain how. He did not ask as he was looking back again when I answered.

I think he just wanted to be sure that we could get in.

This second time of visiting, I turned down to join the riverside road and drove along it to the garage. I stopped. The BMW did not appear. I thought it would be waiting round the corner of the turning we had come down.

We got out. I locked the car and we went in through the garage and the garden. I had locked the garden door on leaving by closing it sharply and used a key to open it. I pushed the door wide open and listened.

'What's the matter?' he said.

'I thought I heard something, but it must have been out on the road.'

I went in and he followed. He looked all round him as if deliberately looking for something wrong.

'The axe is missing,' he said, as we came into the hall. He looked round again as if expecting to find something else missing.

'What are you looking for?' I said.

'I don't know,' he said, and frowned. 'It just doesn't seem the same. Something has changed.'

I leant against the newel post at the foot of the stairs and watched him. He went into the other rooms, looked in the kitchen and then came back, shaking his head.

'Something's wrong,' he said, looking round the hall again. 'Something in here.'

'What about the rug?' I said.

'Rug?' He looked round.

I pointed to the rug by the stairs.

'That's it! What an extraordinary thing!' He stepped back towards the garden door, then turned. 'Yes, that's it. A different colour. The other was more of a blue content. This is quite red. Yes. It changes the hall somehow. How did you know? Did you notice it too?'

'I didn't see it before this morning. That rug was here then.'

'Why on earth change the rug?' he said, bending to look closer at it. 'This is Persian, but the colour isn't quite as good. It looks much older, or more worn, perhaps.'

'Perhaps it came from a store-room?' I said.

'Yes. There is a lot of stuff up in the attic rooms. But why change for the worse?'

'Perhaps the other one was bloodstained.'

He looked up very sharply.

'Bloodstained? How?'

'We have already talked about Harrison's liking for imagining murder. Suppose he did one?'

He stared for a moment, then shrugged.

'He couldn't! You know these over-dramatic people. They threaten but they never do. I don't believe they ever intend to do anything.'

He paced to the door and back. I sat down on the stairs. I was very tired and somewhat drained by the events of the past many hours.

'Mr Maclean,' I said, 'you know Mr Franklyn?'

'Harrison's boss. Yes, I know him.'

'He came here last night. The house was empty. He said there was blood on the floor by the stairs and that a large Persian rug, which he'd seen to be always there, was missing.'

'I see,' Maclean said, after a long pause. 'So you think that something really did happen here? But what? And why is a car following us? What has that to do with Harrison?'

'Did he have a lot of visitors? Would you know anything about that?'

'No. I always had the idea that when he was at home he liked them to be alone. Perhaps his jealousy made him tend to keep friends away.'

'Mr Maclean, what sort of woman is Mrs Harrison?'

'I've told you.'

'I mean in her behaviour?'

'A very delightful person. Lively.'

'Was she forward with men, would you think?'

He almost glared then.

'No! I would not say so. She is as I say,

lively. Playful.'

'You keep overlooking the fact that I overheard Harrison talking to you yesterday, when he was baring his soul, and though you say he often did that to satisfy his inner feeling for drama, he may have had a reason for jealousy.'

'Every jealous man thinks he has that.'

'Let's not beat about the bush. Is Mrs Harrison a whore?'

'No!'

He looked as if I had insulted him personally.

'It would be impossible for her to be a call-girl, because that's what Harrison told you she was.'

'He was rambling. I told you that. There was no sense in what he was saying yesterday. I have tried to explain that to you.'

I got up from the stairs. I wanted a drink of water and went through to the kitchen to get one. As I filled a tumbler under the tap I looked out through the window to the garage roof.

Above it the top of a furniture van was backing slowly towards where my car stood.

The hearse had returned. The chill that kept coming over me in that death house enveloped me again.

CHAPTER EIGHT

1

Maclean came into the kitchen while I was standing at the sink, watching the removal van back up to where my unseen car stood.

'This place is giving me the—' He stopped. 'What's the matter? Something wrong out there?'

He came to where he could see out. I turned away.

'It's only a furniture van,' he said. 'What's wrong?'

'It's a hearse,' I said.

'A hearse? That big?'

'It took away a dead body from here not long ago. I was thinking it might have come back for another one.'

He stared at me.

'Do you mean there was a murder?'

I nodded.

'But who was killed?'

'I don't know who he was. I found a letter he'd dropped addressed to a Kelly in Ohio.'

'Ohio? The States? One of Harrison's dealers was he?'

'I repeat, I don't know who he was. I found him when I looked in the cellar. I came back to ring the police. The phone was haywire. Just kept giving an engaged signal and no dialling tone. I went back to take another look so I could describe it more fully, but when I looked down, the body had gone. Then I saw this van pulling away.'

He turned and looked at the door, as if someone might be there.

'Where are the Harrisons? Do you know?' he said, looking back.

'They're at my house. They came in the night. I couldn't get rid of them. They were frightened. My belief is they've got into something that's far too big for them, and now they're scared stiff.'

'What sort of big? What do you mean?'

'I don't know, Mr Maclean. I'm only guessing. What they told me was a rigmarole I believe they invented to hide the real reason why they're too frightened to come back here.'

He looked out of the window again.

'But there's nobody dead here now, is there?' he said.

'Not yet,' I said.

'My God!' he said, and stared at me. 'You surely can't mean they would kill us? What for? Who are they? Why would they—?'

'I don't know any answers. The Harrisons told me rubbish. No one yet has told me the truth. For instance; why did you believe he might murder her?'

'It was the way he was talking. There was something in his whole manner, the tone, the words he chose—all that made me very uneasy. He did ramble sometimes. He often did it. I think it was a kind of mental tiredness, but yesterday there was no sign of it. He seemed dead set on killing her.'

'I thought it might have been said for my benefit.'

He looked at me very sharply indeed.

'What on earth for?'

'If I knew more about the real Mr Harrison I might be able to tell you. As it is, I don't know the reason for anything in this affair. From what's happened today, I think they've got mixed up in some agency business.'

'What's that?'

'CIA. MI5. KGB. That sort of thing.'

His features seemed to freeze.

'Hell, no!' he said, almost choking. 'Surely they couldn't have!'

'Why not? He travels Europe a lot. He might be a courier.'

'Carrying messages? No. He's not watertight enough to be in that. He's too erratic. Surely they'd never involve a man like that?'

'I had the impression that for his sort of dealing a certain poker-player quality is necessary?'

'More swift and subtle cheating than a long bluff. He can't stand a long strain. No. He's not the sort—'

'But what?'

He shrugged.

'Nothing. I was rambling myself then.'

All the time we talked I kept a close eye over the garden, but I had seen no sign that anyone was trying to get through to the house by way of the cellar.

'Harrison is not the sort, but—' I repeated after him. 'But what? But his wife may be?'

'That's absurd!' he said hotly.

'Is it? Suppose she isn't a call-girl but that's a story to cover up the fact that, for her work, she has male contacts at varying times.'

'Mata Hari is dead!'

'But her song goes marching on.'

'It's impossible!' He was very angry. He turned to the window again. 'We ought to go. If there is something evil going on here, let the police deal with it.'

'There's no hurry. If we go out we may be interviewed before we get to a car, yours or mine. That's if what we suspect has some truth in it.'

'I can't take this situation seriously—'

'Mr Kelly did. So did somebody else last night. Some sort of clean-up has been going on in this house, and it's organised by a team which clears up its own mess without bluster or show of aggression.'

'Let's get the police!'

'Wait a minute. Both Mr and Mrs Harrison insisted that they could not go to the police. Now what was the reason? At first I thought it must be the usual one; that they were scared to go. Now I've seen the sort of thing going on in this house I fancy it's not because of a personal fear they won't say anything to the police; it's because they work for the higher department, or perhaps not one of our departments at all.'

'Secret agents!' he said scornfully. 'You can't be serious!'

'How do you know you haven't contacted such people before in business or the club, or at golf? They don't wear long black cloaks and false noses. They look like you or me or Mr and Mrs Harrison.'

I watched him. He began to pace the floor. He was trying to make up his mind about something. I looked at him, then out at the garden again.

No one had appeared so far, yet I was sure that the van was the same one that had driven away just after Kelly had been taken. I was also sure it had not come back for nothing. The top of the van was well above the garage roofs, allowing the whole of the painted word 'Removals' to show. And amongst those letters a spy-hole would easily be concealed.

I felt sure that the van was at the moment watching the house by such a means.

He stopped pacing.

'It's possible,' he said at last. 'Just possible. It takes getting used to. Yes, it could be—but not Jim. I'm sure he wouldn't do it actively.

He's too moody, too much up one minute and down the next. No. But she—It's possible.'

'Then why did she come to me? Why didn't she go to her own bosses? They would have dealt with any difficulty. That's what they're there for. And she shouldn't have dragged in an outside man like me.'

'She always has a reason,' he said. 'A logical reason. And she always smiles as she gives it, as if to make you feel less of a loser when you accept it. She's a charmer.' He looked to the window. 'You can't be right about that van.'

His voice sounded dry when he said the last sentence. He was rattled. I was not as nervous as I should have been, because I could not forget that the van people, whatever their intentions, had covered up my murder for me.

'What if they do come in?' he said suddenly. 'They wouldn't do anything to us, would they? Wouldn't that give them away?'

'Why should it? They'd take away the evidence of whatever they did to us.'

'Do you mean that if we do ring the police they wouldn't do anything about it?'

'I don't know. But if Mrs Harrison is running away from this house, her people will know, and the police may have had a caution about this address, which would make them refer any call about it to a higher rank for decision. It all depends on what this matter is about. If it's international, then they would get advice.'

'Suppose it's just a gang after jewels? He kept a lot here. His firm scatters the stuff about in various places so if there's a robbery, only a small part is lost.'

'Gangs don't normally work like this. They burst in, blow up the safe and rush off, tyres screaming, then try and disappear. Or, if the house is empty, which it was last night, they could just do the job and walk away.'

'Who was dead? You say you saw him, Kelly.'

'He may be called Kelly. An American, but it's only a guess. I'm not sure. I never saw him before.'

He started pacing again, then stopped.

'We can't stay here!' he said, angrily.

'All right, then. Which car shall we go for? It might be safer out front, but it might not be safe back or front—'

I stopped as I saw a man come into the garden from the garage. He was in blue overalls and carried a sheaf of what looked like invoice sheets in his hand. He was alone.

He came quite openly and went out of sight as he climbed the steps to the garden door. I turned away from the window.

'Watch the garden,' I said and went to the kitchen door as a bell rang.

'You're not going to let him in?' Maclean said sharply.

'I'm going to see what he wants. Watch the garden.'

I went out to the back door and opened it. The man looked at his sheaf of invoices.

'Number eighteen. That's right, isn't it? Some boxes to be taken?' He looked at me keenly.

'I don't know. I'm waiting for the owners to come back. Do you know where the boxes are?'

He consulted the sheet again.

'Says here, "In cellar; entry from door in garden".'

'Oh yes. There is a door down there.' I pointed down to the left.

He went back on the step and looked down.

'Bit overgrown, is it? Like to come and show me?'

'I've never seen it. Have a look.'

I certainly did not intend to go down into that overgrown place in front of the removal man.

'No, I meant show me which boxes. Or are there only six down there?' He looked at me.

I knew there were more than six, but I just wanted him to take six boxes and get out of it, now that he knew the Harrisons were out.

I laughed, but not with happiness.

'I'm afraid I don't know. I can't help at all.'

He looked at me, then slowly folded his invoice sheets in half, making a fat packet.

'I'd better wait, then, hadn't I?'

'Is there somewhere else you can go first?'

'No. This has got to be first call. We have to pack the van right, otherwise we lose space.'

Pack the van, I thought; yes, but what with?

2

'It's difficult to know what to do,' I said. 'They may be hours. I'm doing some work here, and I don't know anything about boxes.'

He looked back towards the van as if he might see a signal from it.

'I'll hang about,' he said, turning back. 'They may come back. No good taking the wrong things.'

'Exactly,' I said, thinking he'd go to the van.

But he didn't. He stood there as if expecting me to ask him in.

'I must get on with my work,' I said. 'You hang on if you like—'

At that moment, just as I was going to get free of him, the front door bell started to ring. One of those old waves of cold ran right through me. Once more I was frightened, and a feeling of emptiness inside made me feel rather sick.

I nodded to him and then shut the door. He watched me steadily through the panels as

I locked the door and turned away.

As I started down the hall I saw Maclean standing just inside the kitchen doorway.

'There's somebody at the front!' he hissed. 'We should have got out! What the hell can we do now?'

'How do I know? I don't even know what's going on! I should have expected you to know more than me. At least you know the bloody Harrisons, which is more than I do!'

'Is there another way out?'

'Through the sides, but I didn't see any doors. Look, shut up. We must treat it calmly or be bust. The man at the back pretends to be genuine, so he's not sure of us.'

'What do you mean? He might be scared of us?'

'Why not? He doesn't know who we are. He can't know who I am, anyhow, even if he might have seen you here before, he hasn't seen you yet.'

The front door bell rang a second time.

At the garden door I could see the haulier watching me as I went on down the hall to the front door. In my head I had the same excuse about my being there that I had given to the haulier. Then I realised that the caller might be someone useful, like a policeman come to enquire about Harrison's driving licence.

When I opened the door a man stood there, a quiet, silent man in dark suit and bowler hat with a look of infinite artificial sympathy on his face.

He bowed his head slightly and then removed his hat as if to come in, but stopped hat in hand when I interrupted his assumption.

'Who are you?' I said.

He looked startled, then from his waistcoat pocket produced a business card.

'An undertaker?' I said, but not very loud because my throat partially froze up at the implication of the visit. I recovered. 'I think you've mistaken the address.'

'No one requiring our services?' he said, surprised. 'I have the right address. I see the number by the door is eighteen. Surely—?'

His quiet deference did not seem shaken by the confusion.

I looked past him to the green opposite. A man was standing by the tree where I had first seen Maclean, and he was watching us. There was a car parked in among others along the kerb to the right of the house. There were two men sitting in it, watching us.

'If this is a hoax,' said the undertaker, quietly, 'I'll tear his bloody ears off. I'll screw the bugger down in one of my strongest boxes and send him to the crematorium.' He spoke in a quiet even voice all the time, and then raised his hat. 'I thank you, sir, for taking my error so politely.'

And he went away. I closed the door and

turned round.

'There are three men watching out the front,' I said so Maclean could hear. 'And we don't know how many are at the back.'

'Get a policeman here,' he said, evenly but tensely. 'Say you think the house has been broken into. Tell them any old cock-and-bull so one turns up. We can go away with him.'

It was a good idea. The problem was to find what sort of story would bring one and would not get us arrested.

I did not want to be arrested. Kelly's death weighed heavily on my conscience though I believed in my total innocence as to intention.

There was nothing for the police to find about Kelly, his visit or his death and departure, but it was not a matter on which I felt easy.

I remembered too well Poe's murderer in *The Tell-Tale Heart* who gave himself away through his bad nerves making him hear the beating of the dead man's heart.

'All right,' I said. 'But what story? Suspect a burglary? And what's going to happen if the police have had a warning and refer the matter to somebody who'll come along and wipe everybody out, us included?'

'Imagination. It couldn't happen. Just think of something mild that will bring one.'

The front door bell rang again. We looked at each other.

'What comes after undertaker?' I said to

myself and sat down on the stairs.

The bell rang again, two rings. It sounded imperious.

'You go,' I said. 'It's probably the embalmer.'

He came out of the kitchen door at last.

'The man at the back door,' he said in a whisper as he came alongside, 'he's gone!'

'I don't suppose he's gone far,' I said. 'He promised to wait.'

The bell rang again. Maclean eased his collar from his neck with a forefinger, then went and opened the door.

There was a police constable outside.

'Mr James Harrison?' the policeman said.

'No. He's not here at present. I'm a friend.'

'Do you know where he is, sir?'

'I don't. No.' He turned and called to me. 'Do you know when the Harrisons will be back? Or where they are?'

'No,' I said and joined him at the door. 'What's the trouble?'

There wasn't much need to ask as the constable held a folded summons in his hand.

'If you had some idea when he'll be back, sir?'

'I haven't. No. I've been working here but he told me not to wait. In fact, I'm just going.'

I passed Maclean and went out on to the step. He almost jumped forward but just held on to the door.

'Hang on. I'll give you a lift,' he said and he came out as well banging the door behind him.

The three of us walked down the steps together. The police car was just down the road and, apparently, so was Maclean's car. So we all walked on together.

We passed the two men I had seen sitting in the car and noticed their stony faces, quite expressionless, as we went by.

We left the constable at his car and went on. Maclean's vehicle was two cars behind. He hadn't locked it. We just got in.

'That was a gift from the gods,' he said, and drew a deep breath as he started up.

For one awful second I waited without breathing as the idea of a bomb having been wired in the ignition took hold of my mind. Nothing happened. We drew away.

Of course nothing happened. The idea of secret agencies and underhand tricks happening in the house had come out with me.

We mixed in with the midday traffic heading back into town.

'We've got out of the house,' I said, 'and that's all.'

'What do you mean?'

'I mean that we're in it now, whether we like it or not. The jolly chaps are probably following now and there's no way they're not going to find out who we are, so don't get optimistic.'

'Then what the hell are we supposed to do?' he said, very angrily.

'Wring the truth out of the Harrisons—if they're still at home. There is virtually nothing else that we can do. We suspect that it's some kind of secret-agent set-up but we don't know.'

'It might be an international gang of diamond thieves,' he said.

'But they wouldn't show themselves to us,' I said. 'They wouldn't have an interest in trying to get hold of us. We don't know anything about diamonds and they would know it. The idea is a non-starter.'

'You're probably right. Our only hope of a quiet life is the Harrisons at your house. Tell me where to go.'

I looked at the traffic behind us. I looked very carefully and as the van immediately behind slowed to turn left it uncovered the car behind.

It was a black BMW.

'Don't do anything foolish,' I said. 'You'll probably crash if you do, but that BMW is right behind.'

He groaned.

'What can we do?'

'Stop at a police station and ask if they serve tea? No. If we stop that car will wait. The question is; can there be any sense in running away when there is always someone running right behind you? We'll never shake them off now. There's something that they want from us, or something we know they want to stop us telling.'

'Shall we stop and kiss and make friends before we're shot?' he said bitterly.

'No. We'll go on to my house, and they'll follow. But going by what they've done till now, they'll just stay by and watch.'

'Then we'll be trapped inside, just as before.'

'We're trapped anyway, dear boy. Out here we can't get away. But once we're in my house we shall have the Harrisons.'

'I see,' he said, eyes gleaming with sudden hope. 'Then we can send them out, and that'll be what these people really want!'

CHAPTER NINE

1

I looked back again. There was another car between us and the BMW. We were driving beside a wide pavement with shops on the inside. I saw a phone box standing between two shops.

'Pull up,' I said.
'What—?'
'Pull up! I want to phone.'

He pulled in to the kerb. I opened the door and got out and as I stood and turned to shut the door, I saw the black car from the corner of my eye. It seemed to hesitate and then pulled out and around us and went slowly ahead in the traffic stream.

I crossed the pavement to the phone box and rang my office.

'I shan't be in till later, Monica,' I said when my secretary answered. 'Is there anything urgent?'

'Oh, that call-girl you wanted. I fed in some more to the computer and it came up with a name and address, but I don't know if it's any good.'

'Just say.'

'Geraldine, The Stern, The Bec, Streatham. It's suburban, like you said, but it doesn't sound a house of the one-in-a-row sort.'

'It'll do. Thanks, dear.'

I went back to the car.

'Change of route, avoiding followers,' I said. 'Next turning right, then right again and over Battersea Bridge.'

'To where?' he said signalling to start away.

'Streatham.' I watched his face. 'Know it?'

He did not seem surprised.

'Not very well,' he said. 'But there's a street directory in the glove-box there. London A-Z. I have customers in strange places.'

I looked it up in the book as we headed south. The road named faced a common, so I thought it should not be too difficult to find. I kept a good eye behind, but did not see the shadow car again.

That it should have been lost so easily was surprising to me. I wondered if it had passed on the job to another car, but no car appeared to follow us for long enough to have been a shadower.

We found the road alongside the common. The houses were mainly old Victorian pieces set back in their own grounds and converted into flats. All except The Stern. That had a black board just inside the garden with rather faded gold paint advertising Miss Pennycome's Dancing and Deportment School for Young Ladies.

'Is that what you want?' he said as we drove slowly past it.

'Just pull up farther on. Tell me, what is Mrs Harrison's name?'

'Well, it was Geraldine, but he changed it to Margaret. Don't ask me why.'

'*He* changed it?'

'Yes.' He looked at me, then shrugged.

'I'll be ten minutes,' I said. 'Do you mind?'

'We're in this mess together. How can I mind? You might find out what's going on. I have no clue.'

I got out and left him staring out at the common. It was then twelve twenty-four. I went in the gate and crunched up the grass-grown gravel of the old drive. I rang the bell. It was opened almost at once by a most magnificent woman of about thirty-five. She eyed me sternly for a moment.

'I am to ask for Geraldine,' I said, hoping I was right.

She eyed me again, then smiled and opened the door wide.

'Come in,' she said.

As we went in I saw a girl and man walk along the landing above. He had his arm round her waist. He wore a dark suit. She wore nothing at all. Their backs were to me and they went into a room and out of sight.

The woman showed me into a room on the right which was most lavishly furnished. She turned then, regarded me again and smiled once more.

'I haven't heard from Geraldine today,' she said. 'She usually lets me know when she has a friend coming because we have no male members, you see.'

'Oh, this is a club?'

'Indeed yes. A group of us housewives got together to form a luncheon club. We entertain friends but by invitation only, so we just have who we want. I'm so sorry I haven't heard from Geraldine.'

'Does she come often?'

She smiled kindly.

'I'm afraid I can't tell you that. Perhaps I

can give her your name when she does call?'

'Mr Keyes,' I said.

'Oh yes,' she smiled again. 'I'm sure she'll be sorry to have missed you.'

I left and went back to the car.

'Well?' he said.

'It's a freelance, part-time brothel,' I said.

He looked back through the rear window at the board.

'Well, let's go,' he said, and went to open the door.

'By invitation only,' I said.

'Why did you go there?'

'I was trying to check that story I overheard, about Mrs Harrison and the call-girl tendency.'

He stayed silent and made no attempt to drive on.

'You're in the business,' he said. 'What do you really think is going on all round us?'

'What have the Harrisons brought us, you mean, probably,' I said. 'I begin to believe that we have landed in the middle of some secret-service activity and it may not be our secret service.'

Again he stayed silent.

'You knew that?' I said.

'I didn't know exactly that,' he said. 'But he told me he was in trouble and needed help.'

'So you agreed to meet him at the pub, where he told the sad story in such clear tones

that I could hear it?'
'Just that.'
'The table was bugged?'
'He knew one would be slipped in there somewhere near him.'
'It was a long shot, surely? He might not have got that table.'
'They waited to see he did. Those heavy glass ashtrays. Each table has one. The waiter takes them and cleans them as they get dirty. I think there was a bug stuck under the one he had. So when he sat down, the waiter dished out the ashtrays.'
'I see. And he told you what to expect?'
'Not exactly, but he hinted. I guessed the rest.'
'He must have known somebody was there listening, because that story was rehearsed, surely?'
'He said there was a porpoise close behind him.'
'Do you know if he was involved in spying? He was abroad a lot.'
'I don't know for certain. He's not a man to tell a lot. Moody, when he says nothing. Happy, when he talks rubbish. Either way you learn very little, except when it comes to his jewels. Then he's verbose.'
The call at The Stern was not fruitless, but it had not found the suburban house which Harrison's story had so firmly put into my mind.

And there was Geraldine, the call-girl. At least I had traced one such, who, it seemed, made her own appointments at Madam Pennycome's, if that was the lady's name.

Such appointments need not have been for the purpose of pleasure. They could just as well have been for the purpose of receiving information, especially as Geraldine made the appointments.

Since the dreadful appearance of Kelly and its worse outcome, I was quite sure that some international force must be at work, and no other form of syndicate ever cleans up bodies in such a very clean and scientific way as Kelly had been wiped up. The cleaners wished it to be known that Kelly had never been there. The efficiency of their cleaning was frightening, so was the speed with which it had been done.

It surely meant that when I had shot him, somebody had been down in the cellar to begin the clearance immediately I had left the cellar. Yet they had not threatened me. Their purpose had been to get rid of Kelly's blood and body and pretend he had never existed there.

In which case they must have been prepared for any eventuality, and had not harassed me because they recognised that I was on no international account. I was grateful for my inferior standing in their affairs.

Maclean started the engine, then switched it off again.

'Look back,' he said, staring up into the mirror.

I did. Miss Pennycome was walking along towards our car.

'A smasher,' Maclean said, with a short whistle. 'I could care for that.'

The woman came up, tested the back door mechanism, then, finding it unlocked, opened the door and got in.

'Are you police?' she said.

'No,' I said. 'I'm just a friend of Geraldine.'

'And the driver?'

'The same.'

'What do you want her for?'

'She's at my house,' I said. 'She wanted me to fetch something from hers.'

'Why send you?'

'She's frightened to come.'

There was a silence.

'I see,' the woman said, as if what I said about Geraldine was not unusual. 'Is she in trouble?'

'I'm afraid so, but I don't know what it is.'

'She thought I would tell you her address?'

'Yes. But when I met you just now I felt you wouldn't tell me.'

'I wouldn't,' she said, 'but this time you are answering my questions. So tell me what it is she wants you to fetch for her and I'll get it for you. We don't give our members' addresses. You probably understand why.'

'Of course.'

'What is it she wants?'

I said the only thing I could think of.

'A fireman's axe?'

'That thing?' She shook her head in puzzlement, then went on, 'Drive back and into the front. I'll run the errand while you have a drink.'

Maclean drove back and up the drive. We followed the magnificent person up the steps and into the luxurious room.

There were two young women standing there by a drinks table. Miss Pennycome introduced them as Mrs Green and Mrs Hayward. Maclean straightened his tie. The magnificent madam left us. Mrs Green gave us drinks. Mrs Hayward interested herself in Maclean and asked him about himself. He said he was a naval architect.

We all sat down. Mrs Green was very charming. The time passed quickly until the magnificent woman came back.

'I must speak to you,' she said to me, and signalled to the girls with a slight motion of her head. Mrs Hayward kissed Maclean and said, 'See you.' Mrs Green just gave me a look that made me sorry for the interruption. Both went out.

Miss Pennycome closed the door.

'Geraldine is dead,' she said. 'Murdered

with that bloody axe. I always felt something dreadful would happen with that thing lying about.'

2

'Where was she?' I asked.

'In the hall. It looks as though she answered the door to someone, who then shut it again and went.'

'Her husband was living with her, was he?'

'Yes. If you call it living. They didn't get on.'

Maclean just stood and stared at us, as if in a state of shock.

'Have you a photograph?' I asked.

The woman hesitated, then said, 'Yes,' and turned to what looked like a Sheraton cabinet, but what was in fact a disguised filing-cabinet. She found a picture and handed it to me. 'Why do you want to see it? Sentimental reason?'

I looked at the picture.

'That isn't the Geraldine I know,' I said. 'There is some mistake here. I'm sorry. Have you told the police?'

'Not yet,' she said. 'I don't want my house connected with her murder. You understand?'

'Yes. You're going back there?'

'When I've had a drink.'

'Would you like me to come with you? I've seen some of this sort of thing before.'

She stopped in the act of pouring a stiff Scotch and looked round at me.

'You said you weren't police.'

'I'm not. But I have been somehow involved, and I want to know what I can expect if the police come to me.'

She eyed me critically, then nodded.

'All right.' She looked at Maclean.

'Must get back to my office,' he said. 'I've been out of my routine today.' He looked at me. 'Ring you later,' he said, with an odd sort of stare.

He went. I left with Madam.

'My name is Frances,' she said, as we got into a nondescript-looking car of popular make but unpopular date. 'I use this banger like a plain van, if you understand. It's quite a job protecting the good name of a freelance house, but it's fun.'

'And profitable?'

She did not answer that.

We drove into a road lined with fairly modern small detached houses. She stopped in a side road and we went round into a back alley which served the backs of the places. There were a number of dustbins waiting there for emptying.

She went in at a door in a garden fence and we walked up a small garden with high hedges; high because they were overgrown.

'What does the husband do?' I said quietly.

'Something to do with jewellery. She

doesn't—didn't talk much about that.'

She opened the back door with a key. It opened into a small kitchen. She crossed it and went into the hall. Then she stopped.

I came up behind her. She stayed quite still a moment looking down the hall, then turned suddenly, looked at me with wide eyes, then closed them and grasped my arms as if she might collapse and needed a hold.

I couldn't see round the edge of the doorway.

'What's the matter?'

She whispered so that for a second or so I didn't quite make out what she said.

'She's gone!' she repeated.

The cold feeling I'd suffered several times at Hampton Court came back in full force then.

She recovered, let me go and turned to go into the hall. I followed her. The place looked as if it had just been cleaned.

'I saw her there, lying by the front door. The—the pointed end of the axe was in her head. I didn't dream it.'

She looked at me steadily as if to see if I believed her.

'Was there much blood?' I said.

She made a small grimace, then shook her head.

'On her hair, but it didn't seem a lot to me.'

'And you're sure she was dead?'

'I once trained as a nurse. I know when someone is dead.' She looked round again. 'What the hell's happened? If I wasn't so sure of myself I might think I was going mad.'

I knew very well what had happened. To me it seemed to be happening all over the place.

'Shall I make sure nothing's here?' I said.

'Please!' It sounded heartfelt.

I passed her and looked into the rooms, one after the other. None was as tidy as the hall, but all were empty of people, alive or dead. A spare bedroom had not been tidied at all since someone had slept there. Perhaps that had been the husband's room.

By contrast with the Hampton house, this one was scattered with correspondence of all sorts lying about anywhere, so there could have been no doubt as to the name of the people living—or dead—there.

I rejoined Frances in the hall and saw a fireman's axe hanging in its holster on the wall, its blades polished bright as silver.

'You don't remember if that axe was there when you came in?'

'No, dear. It was in her head. I told you!'

'Don't be cross with me. I'm just trying to help.'

'She isn't—here?' She looked up the stairs and then at me.

'Nobody's here. Everything has been cleaned up in the hall but nowhere else.'

'I can't believe this!'

'It helps you, doesn't it?'

'Well—as far as one can see—yes, of course it does. But why? And who? It's inexplicable.'

'Did you come in the back way when you found her?'

'Yes.'

'You didn't notice if there was a furniture van out the front?'

'As I drove away. I passed the end of this road. Yes, there was a removal van, but I think it was still moving.'

So it had been the same funeral directors as for Kelly, but the manner of the murder did not seem to fit. On the face of it to use the axe would have implicated the husband, but to do that the body must have been left.

Instead the body had been taken, everything cleaned, including the murder weapon, and the husband thus left free.

Nothing seemed to fit anything else, but then I don't understand the complex ways of international espionage. As far as I had seen it was an involved system of cross, doublecross, triplecross and on to infinity, so that nobody trusted anybody, specially not one's own side.

'There isn't another Geraldine, is there? One of yours, I mean.'

She shook her head. 'No.'

'Margaret?'

She shrugged.

'There is?'

'Yes. But she is a rare visitor. She also picks and chooses. Perhaps more so than Geraldine. We don't know her very well.'

'Does she live at Hampton Court?'

She cocked her head.

'You know an awful lot, Mr Keyes. Who are you?'

'I'm a man who's become involved in somebody else's troubles, and I'm beginning to think their troubles are far bigger than anything I've been used to. I don't like it. To be quite honest with you, I'm frightened.'

'Snap,' she said. 'I've had a feeling things were getting a little tense around me, and it wasn't the usual anxious moment about being closed down, but something quite different and much more alarming.'

'Can you tell me what?'

'A man came one day and went with Margaret. When he left I happened to look out of the window and when his car turned into the road from the back of the house here, a car waiting down the road started up and went after him. It wasn't a police car. I do know that. I told Margaret and she wanted to know what kind of car it was that followed.

'A few days later a middle-aged man came and went with Geraldine. Apparently they didn't, but just sat in the room, drank and talked. When the man went he was very taut, I thought, nervous. When he drove away a car followed him.'

'Did you ask Geraldine who he was?'

'Yes. She said he was an importer of things from Poland and Hungary—you know, the satellite countries. There are such a lot of international dealers—' She turned away towards the kitchen. 'I want to go. I have a feeling. Never mind. Just leave with me.'

We went out by the dustbins and got in the old banger. We drove away by back roads to the back of the School of Deportment.

'Why did you come to me?' she said when we got out.

'Margaret is at my house.'

'Are you sure?'

'As certain as I can be.'

We went in at the back of the house the way we had come out. Mrs Hayward came down the stairs wearing only a G-string.

'Frances,' she said, 'I've got a feeling the house is being watched. Should I give the alarm to the rest?'

'Not yet. Why do you think that?'

'There's been a furniture van parked out there for the last twenty minutes, just doing nothing at all. I think there's a camera in it.'

We went into the luscious front room. We could see through the fine lace curtain, though I doubted that anyone would see in through it.

'You see?' said the naked housewife.

I saw only too well. It was Kelly's bloody

hearst that had parked outside. I recognised the writing of Removals along its top side.

CHAPTER TEN

1

I once had a dream of guilt where I was in a house with the front door ahead of me and the back door right behind. Nemesis stood at both, so when I turned to run from her at the front door, she was standing at the back.

'Do you think they're spying?' Mrs Hayward said.

Frances looked at me, saw my expression and turned to the girl.

'Just leave us a moment, Mrs Hayward.'

It was an extraordinary way to address a lady with nothing on who was there to enjoy an increment in her pin-money, and despite the tension brought by the sight of that villainous van I almost laughed.

The girl went out. Frances turned to me quickly.

'What is it?'

'It's the van that's been collecting dead bodies,' I said. 'Your suspicion about cars following some of your customers is right, and it isn't police. At the risk of seeming over-colourful, it might be the KGB or something like it.'

'For us? Why—'

'You and I must get out of here now. Ask Mrs Hayward to carry on the business as usual. Say we must go—any excuse she'll take as normal, and set her mind at rest about cameras. It isn't a police raid.'

'What are we into, for heaven's sake?' Frances said and for the first time showed some severe agitation rather than shock. 'What can we do?' The last question was firm as if the upset in her was under control again.

'We must get out of here. They want me, and they'll want you now, because you know that Geraldine was murdered and the body taken away in that van.'

'Then why have they brought it out there? Supposing I rang the police—' She stopped as if realising the absurdity of the proposal.

'You wouldn't,' I said, unnecessarily. 'They know that. They also know your customers come and go by the back alley and the garage there. They'll be watching that. Can we see down to the road from the back of the house?'

Without a word she led me through into a small back room at the end of the main passage. From there we could see over into the alley and along to the road.

There was a Cortina parked right across the alley entrance.

'They've blocked it,' she said.

'If we try and push that aside with your

banger, we might not be able to drive on. Have you got anything stronger?'

'I have a Range Rover in the garage. I use it to get down to my farm.'

'That'll do it,' I said. 'Let's get down there.'

'We can get into the garage without being seen in the alley,' she said, as we went out of the room. 'I'll tell Mrs Hayward to take over.'

She came back very quickly. We went down to the basement, out across the garden and through a door in the brick garden wall straight into a garage. She got into the Range Rover.

'Would you like me to drive?' I said.

'No. I like a good bash. I only hope that car really does belong to the furniture-van mob.'

'Who else would park like that?' I said. 'Start up. I'll open the doors.'

I did that and she drove up to me. I got in and we went away past the parked cars in the alley and came into view of the Cortina. There was a man sitting in it.

'Get it in the front wheel,' I said. 'Hard.'

She nodded. I watched her firm, determined profile. She was very beautiful indeed, and, I thought, tremendously strong in character, which made me think her rather less feminine than I might have done.

We were doing quite a lick when we came out of the alley mouth. I saw the Cortina driver look towards us and suddenly realise what was going to happen. He reached out to switch on and, I guessed, back out of the way. In fact he had started to move backwards, when we hit him. There was a crash and a scream of rubber across the road, and then we swept round in a majestic curve and sped away up the street as if nothing much had happened.

When I looked back I saw the Cortina slewed right across the road, almost facing the other way. The corner we had hit was mashed right up almost into the engine so the driver wouldn't be able to steer it that day.

'Okay,' she said. 'Now where?'

'First right, then left, across the main road, then left and make it in and out to Westminster Bridge.'

'I know a way,' she said, and took it dextrously. 'But what do we find when we get there, wherever that is?'

'When we get there we will be in my house and there I think we shall find Margaret Harrison and what passes for her husband.'

She looked aside at me in surprise.

'You've got her in your house?'

'She came to my house. I didn't want her. Then her friendly husband turned up. In fact they haven't left me alone since yesterday. It's been a nightmare.'

'Why didn't you call the police?'

'It's not an offence for somebody to call, get let in and then tear your heart out with stories of torment and distress. You can't call the police for that.'

I didn't mention the blank shot he had fired at me. I wanted to forget that gun altogether, although I still had it uncomfortably in my pocket because I hadn't the courage to drop it about somewhere for fear wiping it didn't take all the fingerprints away, and that Kelly's body might—just might—turn up in the Thames someday.

'You're a sucker for sad stories?' she said.

'When pretty women tell them. Not otherwise.'

As we crossed the bridge she asked where to go. I directed her until we came to a large garage set back from the pavement.

'Drive straight into the garage where it says "Service Only".'

'But I don't know this place.'

'I do.'

I opened the window as we drove in amongst the cars and ramps and assorted mechanics. She stopped. I called out of the window.

'Hey, Charlie.'

The foreman came forward, grinning as I got out.

'Give us an estimate for the dent,' I said. 'We'll be back tonight.'

'You must be into business as a dent-collector,' Charlie said and laughed as he eyed my companion with a quietly lustful eye.

'I'll have Hicks look at it.'

We walked out of the side door into an adjoining street.

'Will Margaret be surprised to see you?' I said as we walked.

'Maybe. She's a quiet one. I've never got on with her.'

'You didn't see much of her, you said.'

'No. That is, I didn't. She used the house more by arrangement than anything else. A private whore, you might say. Or, from what you told me, maybe a spy as well.'

We walked on. She caught the attention of almost every man who passed us while I kept idly watching the traffic, and sometimes looking back, thinking I might see the black BMW kerb-crawling.

When we had walked for ten minutes, I signalled a cab. We got in and told him to drive us to Hyde Park Corner, but after a while changed my mind and made him drive to near my mews. We got out in a street lined with parked cars. We walked on from there.

'Just who are you?' she said, with increasing interest.

I told her.

'I thought it must be something, the way you confuse where you're going.'

'Isn't it wise?'

'Sage, even. I'll murder Margaret when I do find her, getting me mixed up in this kind of bloody business.'

'You've got a good case,' I said. 'And so have I.'

There were five empty cars parked in the mews and nobody about but a cat, who got up from snoozing on my doorstep and walked bad-temperedly away.

It reminded me of the white cat which had got in the night before and which had made me think it had nipped in alongside some illicit caller.

I used my key and opened the door. I stood there a few seconds, listening, then ushered my companion inside. I looked up and down the mews before closing the door.

She stood and looked round my living-room.

'I see no Harrison,' she said.

'I'll look.' I went out and into the kitchen. Nobody was there.

I looked at my watch and was surprised at the time. A quarter to three. I compared that with the electric clock on the cooker. It agreed with the watch. I went out and upstairs and looked into the rooms. They were all clean and tidy, as if Mrs Brown had been already, but normally she came at two and was never done before four.

I went downstairs and looked in the usual places to see if Mrs Brown had left a note to say how she had got everything done so early. In the living-room Frances was sitting elegantly in a big chair.

'They've skipped,' she said. 'Don't tell me.'

'They've gone back to Hampton Court,' I said, quickly. 'My guess is they've gone there to get the jewellery he keeps in the safe, and with that they'll skip.'

She cocked her head in askance.

'Whose side are they on?'

'I don't think it can be ours,' I said. 'I'm going to Hampton Court.'

'With me,' she reminded me. 'I'm not going to be skewered with a sharpened umbrella while I'm alone.

'I'm out of vehicles,' she said. 'Have you got one?'

'I've got a rather conspicuous small sports car left,' I said. 'We'll use that, but it will leave a difficulty. I've already left my daily car at Hampton Court. I can't drive two.'

'I can drive one, afterwards,' she said, with quiet thoughtfulness. 'That's if the undertakers aren't driving both by then. I'm new to this sort of thing. What are the chances of survival?'

'The only chance, I think, is to find out the whole secret, and then retreat quickly. They don't waste time chasing; they get out of the country straight away.'

'Are you sure that's what they do?'

'I hope.'

We left the house and got the last available car out of the garage. It was in need of a respray, but any V8 MGB is a mover, perhaps more so with no paint. We made Hampton in very quick time and parked outside. There was no furniture van or BMW amongst the parked vehicles there.

We began to go up the steps.

'You're not going to knock at the door, are you?' she said.

'No. I've still got his keys.'

'Then they're not here yet?'

'Might not be. But she must have keys.'

I unlocked the door and we went in. It was very quiet. She closed the door without making a clack. We both stood still, listening and looking at each other. I thought, 'She must be all of six feet tall,' and tried not to think of anything unpleasant.

I had the feeling I had gone too far this time in my anxiety to clear things up and free myself of the Harrison clutch.

'They aren't here,' she said very quietly.

'Let's look and see if they've been.'

We went into the big front room. There were several pictures on the walls and I looked behind each until I moved one aside and saw a small safe, looking like the breech of a gun.

I let the picture slide back into position then went out and into the kitchen. Everything was exactly as it had been when Maclean and I had left.

'I don't think they have been back,' I said.

'I don't see why they should come back. If they were scared out of your house surely they'd just make a bolt for obscurity? I would, with a mob like that after me.'

'Well, they wouldn't,' I said, staring out of the window over the sink. 'Here they come now. Look, come with me. I want to hear what they say before we bust in on them.'

I took her to the cellar door, opened it, then we both went inside and pulled the door almost to. We waited.

2

We heard them before they came in.

'That's the car he left us in,' Harrison said. 'I watched it from his window. I'm not mistaken.'

'He couldn't still be here,' she said. 'Unless he's dead.'

They broke off arguing on the back step and entered the hall.

'Go ahead and look,' Margaret said. 'We'd better make sure.'

They moved away from the cellar door, but I heard her high heels on the floor not far off. Apparently she waited while Harrison searched round for me. We heard him come down the stairs.

'He isn't here,' he said, breathlessly.

'He may have been carted off,' she said. 'Get the stuff out of the safe. I don't want to hang about here.'

'But what about the house? The furniture? You can't junk it!'

'Look, sweetheart, I can come back. It's you that's got to bolt.'

There was a pause.

'You mean you're going to back out?'

'I mean I don't mind a month or two on the French Riviera, doing nothing on your stolen cash, but after that I come back.'

'I couldn't let you!'

'Don't try and make me do anything I don't want, darling. I'm the honest whore with the heart of gold, remember? I carried your messages. I thought they were to do with jewellery frauds, but you didn't tell me *what* they were. I had only suspicion to go on, and in my heart of gold I had been suspicious ever since Geraldine asked me to do something for her husband. I might have guessed she was trying to shop you and get me to do the dirty work, but, to tell the truth, I fancied you. For a while I thought we could really make it together, profitably, but then I began to think, well if you do come with me, what will you do with Geraldine?'

'I explained all about Geraldine.'

'But you got me to pretend I was scared of being killed. What for?'

'So that this man Keyes could see you were alive. I told you that. Look, Margaret; what's the point in arguing now? We've got to get out—fast. We're taking a risk coming here.'

'You told me to pretend to be frightened. I bloody well was frightened! Somebody *was* in this house last night. I got so scared I ran out and got the car, and that somebody had a bike waiting to follow me! I told you, and you said it was coincidence, just somebody got angry with my driving. Well, we've come back here. The police won't come here, so what are we in a hurry to get away from? Franklyn? No, because he's in this with you. But what about the others? Mac? Are you frightened of him? Or is there somebody in this I don't know about?'

It was becoming very clear that, though the dear lady had been a willing partner in jewel theft on quite a useful scale, she didn't know anything about Harrison's involvement with an unidentified secret service.

Yet he had got her to carry messages, probably in that connection, thus putting her into a danger of which she would be quite unaware.

It was at that moment of eavesdropping that I began to understand that Harrison's treatment of women was callous to a point of planning their destruction.

Certainly Margaret at the moment was not so far from riding away in the furniture van.

'Before we go any further in this, you'd better explain why you don't believe me when I say somebody was in my house last night and that he followed me on that bike. And why didn't he fetch the police as usual when I smashed it up for him, and where's the car I left? Why didn't the police come?'

'I don't know, Margaret! It may have been a burglar—'

'Tell me, Jim, why didn't the police come? Why did you want me to tell a story about being frightened you'd murder me? I know what you told me yesterday. It was all part of the skedaddle-with-the-loot plot, to leave false trails and all that. It sounded good then. It doesn't sound so good to me now you're frightened of somebody who's not the police.

'I can see why you wanted me to pass messages to those foreigners at Frances' stylish brothel, if it was all about jewels and making sure they wouldn't be traced and all that. You'd understand that, of course, and I thought I did.

'But who the hell is this third party? Why did you bring Keyes into it? I know you said he had suspicions about the robbery, but how did he get them? It wasn't me, Jim. I've been playing it blind, letting you organise, because I knew I was going to get a half million in old fivers. But after last night I'm not so sure I am going to get it.

'We can run from the police. Okay. But who's this third party you're afraid of now? You haven't been straight, have you, Jim, you bastard? Who are they?'

'Somebody may have got wind. I don't

know. Maybe Franklyn got a whiff of the idea—'

'Got a whiff? Isn't he in it? You said he was!'

'I cut him out. I found we could manage without his licences—'

'You bloody fool! If we go, he'll follow. He knows Geraldine is your wife. He'll go straight to her and get the dope on how much you've been home there, and what's been going on with me and the dealers who came to the bawdy to see me—she knows everything—'

'Except what we're doing now. Shut up, Margaret. I'll get the stuff and we'll go. Standing here arguing isn't going to—'

'*You* hold on and shut up! I want to get my greedy hands on a half million. Yes. I'm like that. Greedy. But I'm far from broke, and it is only greed with me. I can drop it. And if there's a gang I've never seen following me about to cut my throat for my half million, then you can keep it. I'm not taking that kind of risk, brother. I'm not taking the risk of concrete boots. They give me corns.'

'This is no time to start a row! Shut up, you stupid bitch, and let go my arm. I can't open the safe with you holding on—'

The front door bell rang.

A tense silence fell in the house. Several seconds passed, then the bell rang twice. I thought I recognised the tune of command.

The policeman had rung like that on his last call.

The silence went on. The bell rang once more and then it seemed the caller went away. It was apparent that the caller had not heard anything of the argument going on in the house, but it must have been a very close thing.

'It was a copper,' we heard Margaret say, though she kept her voice lower than before. 'What the hell did he want? Nobody's stolen anything yet!'

'Selling tickets for the police ball,' he said. 'Calm down! Take the damn picture. Shove it on the floor. Okay.'

'He's opening the safe,' I whispered. 'I shall have to go out before they run!'

'I'm with you,' she breathed almost in my ear. 'I have the feeling if we don't he'll bump her off and *then* run.'

I felt the same, but I didn't think he'd do it there, but sometime later.

We heard them come out of the room.

'The back way,' Harrison said.

At that point I stepped out in front of them. Both stopped.

'Why the surprise?' I said. 'You knew I had come here.'

'We thought you must have gone,' Margaret said, breathless from shock. 'But I said it was your car out the back. We both said—'

'It doesn't matter what you both said. It seems to me Harrison has been the one doing all the saying. What the hell he told you about what he's up to, I don't know, but I'm beginning to get the idea.

'It was just unlucky for me I happened to sit at the table behind Harrison's yesterday morning. He had a fabricated story to tell Maclean because he knew the table would be bugged.'

'Bugged?' Margaret said sharply. 'Where was this?'

I told her. She looked at Harrison, then back to me.

'But to bug restaurants you have to be big and clever and *in*,' she said. 'Surely otherwise you'd get spotted.'

'These people are big and clever,' I said. 'They can afford to bribe waiters, or blackmail them just when they want to.

'Your lover here knew that a foreign agency was on his tail. He's a spy, this man of yours, Mrs Harrison, and the third party you've just begun to suspect is the KGB or somebody very like them.'

She was shocked so that she could not speak, then after several seconds she managed, 'Go on, please.'

'Harrison was so intent on his broadcast to the unseen listeners he didn't look at the table behind him, where I was sitting, waiting for a business acquaintance. I overheard almost all the tale he told, and it shocked me.

'After I'd left, obviously Maclean told him I had been there. With his training Harrison quickly found who I was, my address, my phone number. He was very anxious to kid me the story he told wasn't true. As you'd been going with him as his wife quite a lot, I was not to know any different when you came and told me you feared being murdered. It fitted in with what I had heard.

'But at the time you came on the second visit, your lover was murdering his wife with an axe, just as he had promised in the story.'

Margaret looked from me to Harrison, then back. She was astounded.

'He's killed her?' she said in disbelief. She turned to him. 'You bastard! You shameless—' She stopped, obviously because too many vocal recriminations were jamming up in her. She ended with a small *'Oh!'* and turned away from us all and leaned against the side of the staircase. It looked to me as if she had had little real idea of what Harrison was intending to do, and she had none whatever of his spy connections.

Frances spoke for the first time.

'I found her body this morning, Margaret,' she said, and went to her.

Harrison was watching me.

'I went to look,' I said, staring at him. 'We went together, this lady and myself, but by then the body had gone and the place had been cleaned up by your friends. You know them, Harrison? You know why they cleaned up your wife's murder for you?'

He did not answer.

'They did it because they didn't want you grabbed by the police and given the protection of a cell. They want you for themselves. And when they get you, Harrison, you'll wish you'd been killed by your axe, because they'll get everything you know. Everything that's now hidden away in your twisted little soul. They'll have it all out, and by then you won't know if you're dead or alive, but you'll wish you were dead.'

He was frightened, but then he turned his eyes suddenly to the glass panel of the back door. I turned and looked.

The man had come back for the boxes. I could see the top of the furniture van just showing above the garage roof.

I did not feel all that easy myself as I saw the man staring through the glass at us. He raised his hand and rapped on the doorframe.

Harrison stared at him.

'Better answer him,' I said. 'He's come to fetch some boxes.'

Harrison went and opened the door.

'Yes?' he said.

'I've come to collect six boxes.'

'Oh yes. The six down nearest the door. It's down the steps—'

'I know where to go,' the man said and

turned. He went down the steps and to the left.

Harrison turned back to me.

'Are you going to call the police?' he said.

'No. There's no evidence of murder.'

He leaned his back against the wall. He was dead white. I have never seen a face so colourless. It looked as if he were dead already. He turned his head sharply and looked down the steps to the garden as the fat man shouted.

'Harry! Here!'

A second man came down the garden.

'Do you know who they are?' I said quietly.

Harrison just swallowed.

'The last time they came, they took away a body—a dead body,' I said. 'Then they went down to Streatham and collected your wife's body. That furniture van out there is really a hearse. It's an odd set-up, don't you think? I wonder what they want the boxes for.'

He was shaking. All the long days of his spying, his living in secret places, his fearing the very shadows he moved in, were coming to an end. The shadows were real at last, and he was dying before they got him, his nerves withering inside him as he prepared to face the end he must have feared so long.

I went away to the two women.

'I think we should go,' I said. 'Just for now, anyway. Mr Harrison has business with these people and we don't want to stand in the way of negotiations.'

We went to the front door. Margaret was crying and looking angry at the same time as I opened the door, but she was well under control when she walked out into the sunshine.

I felt like flying down the steps and rushing away from the whole area just in case the shadows wanted to talk to me.

We squashed into the little car and got away fast.

'Where?' I said.

'Your place,' said Frances. 'I'll feel safer there.'

'It is safer there,' said Margaret. 'And I have a lot to thank Mr Keyes for. He may even have saved me from the axe.'

She had recovered.

'Why were there two axes?' I said. 'Do you know?'

'Yes, I know,' Margaret said. 'He had nightmares of being shut up in places he couldn't get out of. I think he had the same idea during the days as well; being trapped in a fire. He was a born coward, but he frightened himself more than anybody frightened him.'

'Not now,' I said. 'Things have changed.'

We got back into the mews in record time.

'I told your cleaner I'd done it all while waiting,' Margaret said. 'I had to do something to get a rest from that man's nerves. He was very bad. I think it was the waiting. He wasn't so bad once we went out and nobody was there outside.'

'If he hadn't feared I'd overheard his story, he could have done everything he had planned and probably got away with the whole thing,' I said.

'But when he thought he'd been heard, he started improvising, sending you to pretend to be the threatened wife so I would think it hadn't happened.

'He meant to kill Geraldine and then put her in a box and have the van collect it. That's how the van was given his address. He got too shattered when she was actually dead and then rushed to me perhaps with the idea of working up an alibi. He was breaking up by then.

'I think really the trouble was that he knew the porpoise was on his tail, but then began to realise that it was much nearer than he'd thought, and his nerves had had enough.'

'Forget him,' said Frances, taking my arm. 'Let's play.'